Something in the Air

www.**kidsatrandomhouse**.co.uk

Also by Jan Mark:

They Do Things Differently There
Useful Idiots

jan mark
Something
in the Air

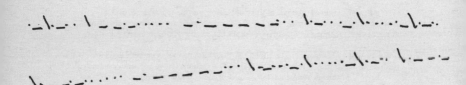

Definitions

SOMETHING IN THE AIR
A RED FOX BOOK 0 09 943234X

First published in Great Britain by Doubleday,
an imprint of Random House Children's Books

Doubleday edition published 2003
Red Fox edition published 2004

1 3 5 7 9 10 8 6 4 2

Copyright © Jan Mark, 2003

The right of Jan Mark to be identified as the author of this work has been
asserted in accordance with the Copyright, Designs and Patents Act 1988.

Papers used by Random House Children's Books are natural, recyclable products
made from wood grown in sustainable forests. The manufacturing processes conform
to the environmental regulations of the country of origin.

Red Fox Books are published by Random House Children's Books,
61–63 Uxbridge Road, London W5 5SA,
a division of The Random House Group Ltd,
in Australia by Random House Australia (Pty) Ltd,
20 Alfred Street, Milsons Point, Sydney, NSW 2061, Australia,
in New Zealand by Random House New Zealand Ltd,
18 Poland Road, Glenfield, Auckland 10, New Zealand,
and in South Africa by Random House (Pty) Ltd,
Endulini, 5A Jubilee Road, Parktown 2193, South Africa

THE RANDOM HOUSE GROUP Limited Reg. No. 954009
www.kidsatrandomhouse.co.uk

A CIP catalogue record for this book is available from the British Library.

Printed and bound in Great Britain by
Cox & Wyman Ltd, Reading, Berkshire

For Margaret Meek

Chapter One

'Open a wee bittie more,' said Mr MacMorris, jovial and coaxing. 'Just a wee bit, that's the lassie. This won't hurt.'

Peggy did not believe him; it always hurt. She did not believe he was Scotch, either. Outside the surgery, she suspected, he dropped the accent as he peeled off his moustache and false eyebrows. She and Hilda had years ago decided that he was not even a real dentist. With that moustache and those eyebrows he looked more like a film villain, one of the American ones who abducted maidens and left them tied across railway tracks for no obvious reason other than that it gave them villainous pleasure and an excuse to twirl their villainous moustaches. The MacMorris eyebrows looked long enough to twirl. As the drill started up again Peggy closed her eyes and ran a private movie in which MacMorris lurked by a railway line where an approaching locomotive belched smoke and the heroine screamed while he twirled his eyebrows.

But being in a dentist's chair was too much like lying helpless across a railway line, and being cut into three by the train could be no worse than the awful grinding of the drill tip into the tooth. It was worse than last time. It was worse than the weeks of toothache that had finally driven her here. The tooth, on its own, second in from the left, had never hurt as much as this. When he paused she would tell him that she had changed her mind, that it was all a mistake, that she needed nothing more than clove oil to cure her in seconds.

The drill stopped.

'You know, screwing your eyes up like that doesn't help a bit,' Mr MacMorris said. His own teeth gleamed in the sunlight. Ollie claimed they were false, stolen from his victims under gas. 'Spit. All over, lassie. Now we'll put the filling in and you'll be as right as ninepence.'

He had been saying that for years, since the first time she had visited him when she first went to school; which was all very well for a six-year-old. Did he say it to elderly grandfathers too, and to the nobility? 'Spit, Your Grace. You'll be as right as ninepence.' Unlikely. No duke would ever let Mr MacMorris near his teeth.

The filling went in, cold and metallic.

'Bite. How does that feel? Once more. Now, no more biting for twenty-four hours. And no toffees or you'll have it out again.'

She stood up, never certain whether or not to shake hands.

'You know, Miss Hutton, you have beautiful teeth, but you won't be getting any more, now will you? These have got to last.'

He was like a gramophone record with a scratch on it, the same thing over and over again. He had been warning her about second teeth having to last since they first came through. He said it to Hilda and to Ollie. He must say it to everyone, including the mythical duke.

'That's two fillings you've got and an extraction. One

gone, twenty-seven to go. Take care of the rest. You'll be getting your wisdom teeth next. Och, the roots on *them . . .*'

Hilda was in the waiting room reading the *Illustrated London News*. Behind her hung a grim oil painting, *The King's Last Stand*, a stag at sunset with the hounds at his throat. MacMorris must keep it there to put his patients in the right frame of mind – abject despair.

'Ready to go?' Under her breath she said, 'What's the Highland Butcher done this time, pulled it?'

'Filled it,' Peggy said. 'It feels as if he soldered it in.'

'Getting his own back for that time you kicked him in the stomach, I dare say.'

'That was eight years ago. I didn't mean to; it wasn't my fault. Fancy taking a kid to the dentist and making believe nothing would happen. He ought to be used to getting kicked in the stomach, it must come with the job.'

'Do you want to take the bus home?' Hilda said, on the stairs. They came out into the street through the doorway between the fishmonger's and Lipton's grocery.

'Not worth it, I'm all right now. Once my face stops aching I'll be able to enjoy my tooth not aching. I wonder why dentists always hide upstairs, over shops. They all do, hadn't you noticed?'

'So no one can look in and see the ghastly things they're doing. Anyway, if we're going to walk we'd better buck up. We don't want to be late for tea.'

'Don't care if I am late for tea,' Peggy said. 'I mustn't bite for twenty-four hours. It'll just be bread and milk for me.'

They cut through the park where mothers and nurses

were rounding up children from ball games and hoop races, to herd them home for tea, as if tea at five o'clock, like evensong at six-thirty, were ordained by God or at least the Archbishop of Canterbury. Was every member of every family in the country eating tea at five? No, not the fathers, hurrying home on trains from the City; not the office girls and shop assistants; not the ex-servicemen who played in a trailing band along the gutters or tried to sell matches and bootlaces from trays in the street. The one-armed man whose pitch was outside the post office had a beautifully lettered card attached to his tray: *My brother John fell at Mons. My brother George was gassed at Cambrai. My brother James was lost at Passchendaele. 'And I only am escaped alone to tell thee.' 1 Job 15.*

Peggy never needed to buy matches or bootlaces and she was too shy to stop and ask him about those lost brothers, John, George and James, to find out what his own name was and ask to hear the tale that he alone had escaped to tell; if he would tell it. The few men she knew who had come back from the war would tell no one anything.

Nor would the women. Aunt Stella had been a VAD, nursing in France. All she would say was, 'Let it settle. One day I'll write about it, perhaps.'

That was the only way to find out, by reading; the poems, the books, to try to *see*, and see without trying the names, the lists of names, cast on bronze plaques on the flanks of Hanstead's new war memorial by the park gates. They were coming to it now, with Daddy's name on the south side, last of the Hs: A. F. Hutton, 12 Battalion Rifle Brigade.

Once, being late for tea had involved facing a scolding Nurse, a sulky maid and rumours of mutiny in the kitchen. Now it meant only that tea too would be late, for they were the ones who made it. Cook had gone off to work in a munitions factory and never returned; the last of the maids had become a bus conductress and married a driver old enough to be her father – old enough, that was, to be still alive to marry her. Nana had gone to another nursery.

It would have been difficult to keep any of them on after Daddy died at Passchendaele along with the match-seller's brother James and thousands, perhaps hundreds of thousands, of others. Mother had moved them all from the big villa in Bedford Avenue to another one in Gladstone Road. It was exactly the same shape and had the same number of rooms, but the Gladstone Road house was joined on to the ones on either side and the rooms were approximately half the size of the ones at Bedford Avenue, as if it were a duplicate that had shrunk in the wash. The garden had shrunk the most, from a lawn and herbaceous borders and roses and apple trees on three sides, to a strip of grass at the back with a path and a flowerbed on either side of it and a single surprising quince tree at one end. Beyond the fence, below the quince tree, at the foot of a shallow cutting, ran the railway line to London. The bank of the cutting baffled the clangour of the trains, which announced their passing with mysterious bursts of steam like Indian smoke signals. No maidens were ever tied to those tracks by villains with MacMorris moustaches.

'I suppose you're too poorly to get the tea,' Hilda said, letting them in with her own key. 'We've all had teeth filled. You don't have to carry on like a dying duck in a thunderstorm.'

She hung up her hat. Peggy bowled hers towards the hall stand with an expert flick of her wrist and missed, as usual. She could remember Daddy doing it, his coming-home-from-the-office trick with his bowler hat. But when he tried it with his infantry cap, after he joined up, he missed for the first time ever.

'Balance is all wrong – it's the peak,' he had explained. 'I'll improve with practice.' But he never had perfected the trick with the cap. He had come home only once again after that, in no mood for tricks.

'You'll ruin that hat,' Hilda said, over her shoulder, at the kitchen door.

'Won't need it much longer,' Peggy said. 'Once term starts it will be back to the pudding basin.'

'Yours doesn't even look like a pudding basin, you've pulled it about so much.'

'It's a wreck and a ruin. I swear Ollie takes it over to the links and collects golf balls in it. Won't Mother stand you a new one when you go up into the Sixth, just for the look of it? Dignified, you know. Then I can inherit yours.'

'And wreck that.' Hilda was at the scullery sink, filling the kettle from the cold tap, which made the water pipes shudder and honk dolefully all over the house. 'There's nothing wrong with my hat. If Kaiser Bill makes me a sub-prefect I'll get a new ribbon for it, that's all.'

'Oh, she's sure to make you a sub-prefect,' Peggy said. 'And won't I just know about it,' she added under her breath.

'I heard that. Yes, you will just know about it if you don't buck your ideas up. Well, *are* you going to play invalids or are you going to lay the table?'

'Mother won't be home till after nine – can't we eat in the kitchen?'

'You can still lay the table. Ollie's enough of a yahoo without letting him think we can just let ourselves go when Mother's not here.'

Make you a sub-prefect? You were born a prefect, Peggy thought. Her jaw ached right up to her left ear. If Hilda had any tact she would never expect her to help prepare a meal that she could not eat. She threw a cloth over the kitchen table, scattering the crumbs she had folded in with it after lunch, slapped down plates and cutlery. Hilda was cutting bread, limp, almost transparent slices that peeled away from the loaf.

'Saw me off a doorstep, will you, and I'll have it with milk. Slops for the toothless.'

'You aren't toothless; don't make such a fuss. And if you're going to heat milk don't let it boil over. You can clean the stove if you do.'

The kettle was beginning to murmur to itself on the back gas burner. Peggy turned her face from the buns and biscuits that Hilda was putting out, the jam dish, the honey pot made like a straw-plaited bee-skep with a large china bee on top, and cut her doorstep into cubes while the milk pan heated. Dare she put sugar on it? The very thought, like the jam and honey, sent a sympathetic stab through her tooth. Sugar caused decay, MacMorris had told her so. 'Think of those wretched Tudor ladies, washing their

7

mouths out with honey and rose water,' he had said happily, 'and ending up with *blackened stumps.*'

As she put the bread cubes in a bowl the milk, seemingly dormant, surged up the sides of the saucepan and over the rim, foaming and hissing on the hot stove and filling the kitchen with that strangely unmistakable smell. How could anything so bland and wholesome as milk smell so disgusting when it burned, and why did the smell spread so far so fast? Hilda had gone upstairs for a moment, but the odour of burning followed her. Peggy heard the yell of anger.

What had she to be angry about? It was Peggy who would have to scrub the stove, scour the pan. She banged it down on the draining board and mopped round the burner, which had gone out, mixing the oily tang of coal gas with the scorched milk. If only they still had someone efficient to do all this. Cook had never burned the milk before she hung up her apron for good and went off to Woolwich to make artillery shells.

She rinsed the dishcloth under the tap, thoroughly, knowing from experience what stale milk smelled like. A terrible miasma had haunted them for days at Easter until it was traced to a floorcloth, stiff and stinking over a pipe under the sink, and Peggy knew who had hung it there. She left the pan soaking, the milk cooling in the bowl of bread, and went down the garden to call Ollie, pausing on the way to peg up the cloth on the washing line outside the back door.

She did not know for sure where Ollie was but she could guess. Mother and Hilda sighed and said that he was running wild but Ollie did not run so very far. On the other side of the railway was a wide strip of rough ground, lumpy with grass tussocks and overgrown with bramble and hawthorn and, in autumn, one brilliant spindleberry, an exotic beacon that signalled across the cutting to the golden light bulbs of their own quinces. Beyond that lay the golf links where slow-moving men, and sometimes women, passed to and fro pursuing little white balls.

Ollie and several other boys in the street had camps and redoubts and supply lines in the rough. As most of them were Boy Scouts or Wolf Cubs they always had the excuse that they were honing their outdoors skills and they were never seen without long sticks which they called staves and which they used mainly for whacking the bushes or bringing down conkers. A good part of their time was devoted to collecting stray golf balls, which they often managed to find before they were lost. Their outdoors skills prevented them from being seen and the balls could be returned to the club house for a consideration.

Some mothers and sisters, as five o'clock approached, made the mistake of going to the ends of the gardens and calling, and soon after a sheepish procession would cross the footbridge at the end of the road, furious with loss of face: Billy, Tommy, Kenneth, Willie dear, Anthoneeee! Peggy was better trained. Ollie had taught her to whistle in Morse code: three dashes, O for Ollie, and dash, T; dot, E; dot dash, A. When Mother was home he too crossed by the footbridge, but on evenings like this when she was working late at the library, he came through the wire on the other side, down the bank, across the line and over the fence.

She did not feel like whistling under her own steam this evening, her lip still sore from MacMorris's spit-sucking machine, and carried Ollie's own whistle which he kept on a lanyard as part of his scouting equipment. Because tea was late she was alone at the end of the garden, all the other humiliating ululating females having gone to their teas already with their sullen sons and brothers. Peggy raised the whistle and blew the requisite blasts, watching for a reciprocal disturbance among the bushes. It was almost half past five – surely Ollie's stomach would have been sending him its own coded signals by now. She looked down involuntarily to the railway line in case he had tried to cross already and misjudged the speed of an oncoming train, timing his transit at the wrong moment. The call to tea fell conveniently between the 4.50 up and the 5.07 down, one still gathering speed as it left the station, the other already decelerating. She did not expect to see his mangled body there but she always felt guilty knowing, as Mother and Hilda did not, about Ollie's potentially lethal short cut.

He was not dead on the track or beside it. There was no stir among the bushes in the rough. Instead she had just time to become aware of a movement in the rhubarb leaves by the corner before a phantom hand swatted the floppy bow that fastened her hair at the nape of her neck, with a jeering yell of 'Flapper!'

'Ollie, you little rotter! How long have you been there?'

Ollie looked aggrieved. '*Hours.*'

'That means ten minutes, I suppose. Serves you right.'

'Why's tea so late? I came across when everyone else did. I *saw* you at the window. Why didn't you call me, I'm starving.'

'You should have come in, then. You don't have to wait to be called. Come to think of it, there's nothing to stop you getting the tea yourself.'

'Women's work,' Ollie said, evidently quoting one of his friends, or the father of one of his friends. It was not an opinion he would have dared to voice in the bosom of his family, where he was outnumbered three to one – four or sometimes five to one when Aunt Stella came to visit, bringing reinforcements – and the shortest by several inches. Peggy did not condescend to answer. Ollie's skills did not include level-headed debate.

'Well, tea's ready now,' she said, 'not that I can have any; I went to the dentist. That's why we're late.'

'Ho!' He was not sympathetic. 'There's a tribe in Africa where they knock teeth out if they give any trouble. No gas or anything, just *whack!* I bet they didn't have dentists at Mafeking.' Owing to his scouting connections Ollie and his friends were still fighting the Boers and the Zulus, often both at the same time.

'Ollie, go and wash your hands – up to the elbows. Peggy, don't forget you've got that milk pan to clean.' Hilda was issuing orders before they were fairly in at the scullery door. 'Take those boots off, Ollie. Peggy, your ribbon's coming undone.'

'Oh, dry up,' Peggy snapped. Hilda's voice vibrated through her tooth like another drill. 'If we're such savages why doesn't Mother go on at us like this? Why doesn't

Stella? We do all these things without being told when they're at home.'

'Yes, but they're not at home.'

No, they were not. Mother was at the library until nine this week, Stella was in London and Daddy was somewhere in Flanders. School friends returned to a waiting mother, a maid, even a nurse sometimes, knowing that Father would be in later. Why couldn't she and Hilda be like Jo and Meg in *Little Women*, friends and comrades as well as sisters, so that when Mother came home worn out she could say, like Marmee, 'Glad to see you so merry, my girls,' instead of sighing wearily, 'What are you arguing about *this* time?'

She sucked morosely at the bread and milk while Hilda and Ollie chewed their heedless way through buns and biscuits. She and Hilda had been like Jo and Meg once – not so long ago, either; friends, shoulder to shoulder against the world, sharing books, cracking jokes. It had been Hilda who came up with MacMorris's false moustache theory. What had happened between them?

'If you want to do a good deed for today, Ollie, you could clean that saucepan for me.'

'You burned it, you clean it. Why should Ollie have to run around after you?' Hilda said.

'I did a good deed this morning,' Ollie said. 'I carried Mrs Barton's shopping for her.'

'That must have broken your back,' Peggy remarked. 'There's no rule that says you can only do one good deed per day, is there? Why not do two today and you could bank the second one and have tomorrow off or –' seeing that this did not appeal '– do two good deeds today and then do something really frightful tomorrow – they'd cancel each other out.'

'Don't give him ideas,' Hilda said, as if Ollie might be irredeemably corrupted and dedicate himself to balancing good works with evil ones. 'He's bad enough already.'

She talked over Ollie's head as if he were not there. Ollie, being used to it and fully immunized, did not care and took no notice. Peggy thought it was shocking bad manners and exactly the kind of thing adults did all the time, meanwhile complaining about the awful behaviour of the young, jazz music, flappers, bobbed hair, motorcycles and smoking cigarettes. Hilda, at sixteen, was still young enough to know better, but there she was, angling to be a prefect, and practising crushing remarks and withering glances on her own family.

You'll be calling us Margaret and Oliver next. What are you so scared of? Peggy wondered. Anyone can see you're sixteen, you look older; you have to flatten your bust already, I don't even have a bust to flatten. Do you think the kiddies at school will cheek you? No one ever cheeked Vera Openshaw.

Vera Openshaw had been a school mystery, two years in the sixth form and never made a prefect, in every first team for every sport but never captain of any, liked by everyone except, it seemed, the mistresses, and particularly the head, Kaiser Bill. No one in the lower school could understand it. Peggy had, just once, tried to question Hilda, which was like Private Buggins asking Field Marshal Haig what the Ministry of Munitions was thinking of. Hilda, who loved

Jan Mark

a gossip as much as the next girl, had started to mutter something about Vera being 'not quite' before she remembered herself and Peggy had got a ticking off for interfering in matters that were so far above her head.

Not quite what? Peggy had wondered. Vera was so liked, so loved, no one ever minded doing what she asked even though she was not a prefect, and she only ever had asked, never barked orders. Well, Peggy hoped she was happy now; she certainly must feel triumphant. At the end of last term, on Speech Day, Miss Williams, Kaiser Bill, looking every inch like her namesake except for the moustache, had announced, rather grudgingly it had seemed to Peggy, that Vera Openshaw would be going to London University on a scholarship. Even in this she had refused to fulfil expectations. The staff had wanted her to try for Oxford or Cambridge and her refusal, and the reason for it, had reverberated through the school. 'Oxford only began giving degrees to women the year before last and Cambridge hasn't started yet. Women have had degrees from the University of London since 1878, that's more than forty years.'

Perhaps the school feared a generation of girls who would have the temerity to look down on Oxford and Cambridge as too out of date to bother about. In future, Vera's name would be mentioned only in hushed whispers, or probably not at all. Once girls had left the High School, no matter how popular, or unpopular, or downright notorious, they vanished as though they had never been, as if the walls had opened and they had passed through into an unseen void. No one ever said, 'I wonder how old

So-and-So is getting on now?' They ceased to have any existence except, perhaps, in the personal memories of people who had learned not to share them. Seen in town, they had become women; no relation to the schoolgirls they had been.

While she thought of all this Peggy had been absentmindedly scouring the milk pan with Vim powder, which was better at taking the skin off your hands than milk off a saucepan. In the old days, she had heard, they used brick dust, and the thought of that set her teeth on edge; MacMorris's molar twinged in sympathy.

Ollie had disappeared as soon as tea was over. Hilda was in the parlour at the front, playing the piano as if the piano had cheeked her and was now being put in its place. Take *that* and *that* . . . and *that*, thump thump. Hilda played as she did everything else, firmly, efficiently, far better than Peggy did, but never getting any fun out of it, using the loud pedal too often as if she could not get out of the habit of putting her foot down.

Peggy enlivened her own practising by pretending to be a concert pianist, one particular concert pianist who had given a recital on the school Bechstein and was memorable chiefly for her technique, much heaving and head-tossing. Peggy played very badly and knew that she was unlikely to get any better by flinging herself about at the upright, where she was liable to hit her head on the candle brackets, but at least she enjoyed herself, and it took her mind off the racket she was making. She loved music and hated to hear herself mangle it. Hilda said that she too loved music and listened to it with her head on one side and her eyes closed, but she rarely used the gramophone and was miserly about rationing out the time when Peggy was allowed to play it.

'Needles are *so* expensive,' she said, piously. She could put the kibosh on anything by reminding the others how hard Mother had to work to pay for it; gramophone needles, for instance.

This was rot. Anyone could afford needles even if they hadn't been able to buy any new records since the war ended.

The tooth was still aching, in a sneaky way, letting her think it had recovered and then sending a sudden stab through her jaw. Peggy went up to the bathroom, dabbed clove oil on the tooth and went to lie down. Her room was at the back, out of range of the piano. As they had no servants now, Ollie had commandeered the attic and hung signs on the door at the top of the stairs: KEEP OUT, CAVE CANEM, TRESSPASSERS WILL BE EXECUTED. Whatever he did in there involved thuds and clanks, mysterious rolling sounds as if he were skating, but he would not be home until the light began to go. If she could get to sleep and stop poking around the tooth with her tongue, it might have settled down by the time Mother came home full of sympathy and, with luck, new books.

She drew the curtains. With the sun on the front of the house now the room was restfully twilit. Gladstone Road was a quiet street; few sounds reached her over the roof even with the window open and she was so used to the trains passing in the cutting she no longer heard them.

Birds were singing – she recognized their own personal thrush that would go on trilling in the quince tree long after sunset. Stretching out on the bed she cushioned her aching face on the cool pillow and waited for the thrush to sing her to sleep.

Chapter 2

She could not sleep. What she needed was a really boring book, but to read it she would have to open the curtains or switch on the light. She resorted to her usual trick of playing music in her head, not just the notes but a performance – a whole orchestra, a choir, a quartet, something that Hilda, beating the piano into submission, would never hear, she was sure.

Sometimes she recognized the music as pieces from their own record collection, sometimes she could not recall having heard it before but knew she must have picked it up at a concert, as though she had recorded it in her head without knowing it. How wonderful it would be to have a machine that would do that, playing any music you wanted, for as long as you wanted, instead of two and a half minutes before you had to get up and change the record; a machine that could be switched on and off beside the bed, like the light; playing softly, just for you, songs, symphonies, operas, ragtime, jazz.

It was a rondo now, by Schubert, something she knew well and often tried to play, frustrated because it sounded so simple on their recording of Paderewski. It *was* simple: why couldn't she do it?

And then she was hearing something else, not Schubert's plaintive notes but a quite different noise and from quite a different source. The music she played to herself was from memory – she imagined it, the way she imagined pictures. The new sound was a real sound and she was not imagining it, she was hearing it. From somewhere very close was coming a stream of staccato pulses, very high-pitched, like the top A on a piano, almost tuneless, as if Hilda, downstairs, were tapping it over and over again, very fast; too fast for a piano key.

The Schubert had faded away as soon as she stopped concentrating. She put her fingers in her ears and immediately the thrush fell silent, but the stream of notes went on, higher than the top A; not notes – no musical instrument could make that sound, no human could play that fast. She could see it, not a stream, an endless string ... not notes but tiny round pearls and long jet bugle beads, threaded haphazardly, long, short, long long short, short short short long, dot dash dot dot dash dot–

Morse code.

Mad Morse code, insanely fast – nobody could do it at that speed surely and anyway, if they could, how would she hear it?

But she *could* hear it. She sat up, riddling her ears with her fingers, and immediately the sound stopped. She heard the thrush again, now the only bird voice in the garden. Then she saw how dark the sky had become beyond the curtains. She had been asleep after all.

She slid off the bed – Hilda would have something to say about the state of her skirt – and stood listening. The piano was silent but overhead tempestuous sounds of shipwreck and train crash suggested that Ollie was going to bed, or practising movie stunts. There were voices in the kitchen: Mother had come home. It must be almost half past nine.

Before she went down she put her fingers in her ears again and stood absolutely still, but the Morse operator had fallen silent. She had dreamed it after all, and that horrible jolt of alarm had been for nothing. Since a certain singing lesson last year she had been dogged by the fear that her imaginary concerts might lead to something far less enjoyable.

Miss Platt, the music mistress, had told them about the great composer Robert Schumann, who had also been able to hear music in his head, but not from choice, and ended up tormented by a single interminable note. Being a musician he'd known exactly which note it was. Miss Platt had actually been telling them about his wife Clara, a friend of Brahms and a distinguished concert pianist herself, but all Peggy could remember was poor Robert, driven insane by the music that he could not control or stop. No wonder. Peggy, her own head so full of music, was haunted by the thought of Robert, maddened by that one note. His, it seemed, had been continuous, as if played on a string by a bow of infinite length, but when Peggy had first become aware of that rapid staccato she had thought, Schumann! Would she be condemned to a whole lifetime of listening to that? Beethoven had gone deaf. Was this how musicians knew Hell, through their ears?

But it had stopped, there was no doubt. She went down to the kitchen, where Hilda was making cocoa and Mother was sitting at the table with a stack of books in front of her.

They all had that horrible library binding that made them look like cash boxes, but Peggy knew that the boxes were full of treasure.

Mother looked up as she came in.

'Oh, poor darling, did you have an awful time? Kiss better.'

Peggy wished away the years so that she might have climbed onto Mummy's lap to be kissed better and the kiss really would have taken the pain away.

'*Look* at your skirt,' Hilda said, on cue. 'Don't tell me you lay down without taking it off first.'

At which point the milk boiled over. This was so satisfying, along with the new books and Mother being home, that Peggy was on her way to bed again before she noticed that the tooth had stopped hurting, but as soon as she was in bed the Morse returned: *dit–dit–ditditdit–dit–ditdit–dit-ditdit*.

It was so clear and so real and whatever she did it would not go away. Then it stopped dead, as suddenly as it had begun, and immediately she began to wonder again if she had imagined it.

She did not want to worry Mother by telling her; Mother had enough to worry about, getting by on a librarian's pay and a pension. Hilda would simply scoff and say she had bats in the belfry.

Perhaps other people heard it too, and like her were afraid to say anything. She might try mentioning it to Dorothy when they met, or Stella. She could tell Stella anything.

* * *

21

Before the war Stella had been engaged to a cheery young man Peggy could only just remember, although she did remember liking him very much. She and Hilda had already started calling him Uncle Peter because he was so obviously the other half of Auntie Stella, but Peter had gone off to do his bit, like Brother Bertie in the song, and six weeks later he was dead at Ypres. In 1918 there had been a second engagement to Lieutenant Derek Stokes and the vague idea that the two of them might be brides-maids when the war was over, but they had never got around to calling him Uncle Derek, or anything at all, come to that. Before they could even meet him he too was lost in action and by then Stella was a Red Cross nurse, first in London, then in France.

If Peter and Derek had ghosts they would be hovering over the great military cemeteries in Europe, but there were others – Peggy thought of them as half-ghosts – Peter's parents, brothers, sisters, cousins, who would have become her own relatives through Stella; still living, shopping, working, riding bicycles, playing football, people she might once have got to know well but now would never know at all.

Peter Heaseman had come from a large family, four brothers, two sisters. Two of the brothers were left, and the sisters, but they were all so much older than she and Hilda. Ollie would not even recognize them. But Derek Stokes had had a cousin, Irene. She and Stella had become friends and now shared a flat in London.

Peggy's aim in life was to follow in Stella's footsteps: a career, a flat in London, shared with a friend. She had already chosen the flat, near Baker Street, like Stella's, and furnished it. Although she had not yet seen Stella's new flat she knew her own imaginary one so well that she could picture it at all times of day, all seasons of the year; pale sun shining through a bay window onto a bowl of blue hyacinths in spring, the same window open in summer with a cool breeze stirring the leaves of the plane tree outside, parties on autumn evenings with piles of the latest gramophone records, interesting people in glamorous clothes, smoking Russian cigarettes in long holders and discussing the latest books. Best of all, she saw herself coming home in winter through dark, snow-filled streets, closing the door on the icy blast – the icy blast was very important – and sitting by the fire with supper that the two of them would have gaily prepared together in the little kitchen with its bright checked curtains and blue-striped crockery, and if anyone burned the milk they would just laugh about it; only they never would burn the milk.

The one thing missing from this picture was the best friend. Peggy had to make do with something resembling a dressmaker's dummy wearing rather stylish clothes but ending with a turned wooden finial at the neck. There was some kind of a head, to be sure, but no face. Peggy was not short of friends and Dorothy Prior was without doubt her best friend, but she could never see their faces, not even Dorothy's, on the other side of that fireplace, at the kitchen stove, coming in through the front door with shopping and flowers.

She would always have fresh flowers in her flat.

Girls at boarding schools in books shared studies,

carrying on like married couples and, unlike the girls at Hanstead High School, would stick together as chums for the rest of their lives. Peggy could not imagine feeling that close to anyone, except Stella. That would be Paradise; sometimes she allowed herself to dream that Stella invited her to share the flat . . . but that would involve getting rid of Irene, and Peggy liked Irene very much. Somewhere out there was the One who would share the flat; they just had not met yet.

Peggy counted the years, four more at school – two in the Vth, two in the VIth – university perhaps, although you could not dream your way into that and it would be another three years on top; then freedom. Seven years, half of her life so far. If Mother and the grandmothers, who paid their school fees, were not so fearfully keen on education, she could be working already – most girls of her age did, although she knew perfectly well that the kinds of jobs they had would not lead to flats in Town. Irene was a teacher, Stella worked for the London County Council and they both had to eke out their incomes with private tutoring. In any case she agreed with Mother, Granny Hutton and Granny Holt about education. There were other girls of her age, and Hilda's, with plenty of money and no need to work, who had no chance of escape, who would drift around waiting for a husband, or go out campaigning for one.

'That's how it's always been for girls like that,' Stella had told her once, 'only now there aren't enough husbands to go round, poor things.' Peggy knew that she was thinking of the Heasemans, the potential four reduced to two and the sisters still unmarried in their thirties. And there were Peggy's own lost uncles; between Mother, the eldest Holt, and Stella, the youngest, had been three brothers.

And then there were the Priors, who had mustered six fighting men in 1914 and they had all come home, eventually, more or less whole.

'It was God's will,' Mrs Prior was obliged to say, unable to admit that it was no more than incredible good luck. Thinking about it after hearing that, Peggy's childhood image of God, a kind of composite of Father Christmas and Jesus (who had turned out to look unnervingly like Rasputin), changed into an absent-minded dotard with a pin who went through lists of men, aimlessly stabbing here and there and turning them into casualty lists. She still attended church on Sundays and went through the motions in school prayers, but she knew that no one was paying any attention. Hadn't they all knelt by their beds every night, all through the war? 'Dear God, keep Uncle Eric safe . . . Uncle Michael . . . Uncle Arthur . . .' And, at last, 'Dear God, keep Daddy safe,' for in the end Alan Hutton had joined up, although he need not have done at his age, because he could no longer bear the shame of being out of uniform while younger men died in their thousands.

The pin had, for some reason, missed Arthur, the youngest uncle, and all six of the Priors. But why should Dorothy have her father home from work every night and not Peggy? Mr Prior was nice enough, but no nicer than Daddy had been, or Uncle Arthur. God had gone back later and got him in 1919, with influenza.

Dorothy was lolling on Peggy's bed with a magazine,

one foot tucked under her, one leg dangling. She was enviably, effortlessly, irritatingly neat; when she stood up her frock would not look like a concertina that someone had trodden on. Her stockings were as straight as those of girls in illustrations, as though they had been painted on. She had tiny feet like book girls, too. Peggy was wearing out her canvas gym shoes, which would make anyone's feet look huge, especially at the end of black stockings. She drew hers up under her skirt where she was sitting against the wall on a cushion. Sitting on a cushion felt very Bohemian. There would be floor cushions in the flat and the people who lounged on them would be reading *Vogue* or *Time and Tide*, not *School Friend* and *Our Girls Magazine*.

'It says here,' Dorothy remarked, 'that you can get grease stains out with benzine. What's benzine?'

'Dunno. Something highly inflammable, isn't it?' Peggy said, shortly. Dorothy had an extensive wardrobe. Peggy was happy to admire, and resigned to envying it, but it was not what she wanted to talk about at all. 'Your skirt would be clean but you wouldn't be able to go near a fire.'

'It's a really good article,' Dorothy enthused, undeterred by Peggy's lack of interest. 'It's about all the different stains you can get on clothes and how to get them out. The oddest things – look.'

Peggy uncoiled herself and craned her neck. The article was illustrated with the usual impossibly slender sylphs, waistless, hipless, bustless, sleek as greyhounds, with endless legs.

'Look, it says methylated spirits remove grass stains. My tennis dress—'

'Sounds as if everything's designed to make you burst into flames.'

'Ugly stains on our dresses when we are very hot—'

'Why don't they just say sweat and be done with it?'

'– should be treated with muriatic acid. What's that?'

'Haven't a clue. Ten to one it's either deadly poisonous or something else that explodes. I think that article's a Bolshevik plot to destroy English womanhood. Have they got anything useful – like how to get bloodstains out?'

'Why would we want to get bloodstains out?' Dorothy said. 'It's not as if we were nurses.'

'Well, every month for a start,' Peggy said and, catching Dorothy's uncomprehending eye, hesitated. 'You know.'

'Every *month*?' Dorothy said. 'What *are* you talking about? What do you do every month, cut your throat?'

Peggy looked away, confused, and struck by an uncomfortable suspicion. Surely Dorothy knew – by now. 'Oh, nothing . . .'

'What? Have you got an illness? You never told me. Peg, what is it?'

There was no way out. Why hadn't some adult let Dorothy know what was coming? Stella had taken Peggy aside a couple of years ago and explained everything very clearly. 'Your mother asked me to,' Stella had said. 'She thinks I'd do it better. Apparently Hilda went into fits when she told her – though I'd say that was Hilda, rather than Mary's explanations. Did Hilda think to pass it on to you? No, I thought not.'

'Monthly periods,' Peggy said. 'Bleeding.' Dorothy's face

was ashen. 'It's called menstruation. It's not just me, all women—'

'We're not women yet. Mumsy would never—'

'Mumsy too,' Peggy said, brutally. 'She'd have to, or she wouldn't be Mumsy. Look, Dot, you ought to know this. Do you want me to explain?'

'Bleeding? Every month? *Where?*'

'I could draw you a diagram,' Peggy offered, wanly. She always got excellent marks for diagrams. Why on earth had she mentioned bloodstains? She ought to have guessed that Dorothy would be shocked, but only in the theatrical way that they all pretended to be shocked at the mention of any body part below the armpits. She had not meant her to be *this* shocked; frightened, panicky.

'I don't want a diagram, just tell me.'

Stella had calmly used medical words – ovaries, Fallopian tubes, uterus, vagina – making Peggy realize why Mother had given her the job of explaining. Mother would just have said vaguely, 'Things…' one word for every organ.

'Every month,' Peggy said firmly, 'one of your eggs—'

'*Eggs?*'

Oh, God, Dot was thinking of hens. Did she imagine that she was going to lay an egg every month and sit there clucking over it? It was no laughing matter but Peggy felt the muscles around her mouth tugging mercilessly. She looked Dorothy in the eye; 'Dot, do you know where babies come from?'

Dorothy, now scarlet, pointed to somewhere around her middle. Well, that was a beginning.

'They grow there, from eggs – *tiny* eggs. Do you know

how they get started? How they come out? Look, my aunt's coming here tomorrow. Why not drop round and she'll explain. She'll do it much better than I can,' Peggy said, with some truth. *Coward*, said a voice in her head.

'What does she know? She hasn't had a baby.'

'No, but she could. All women can, well, nearly all. Once you've started your periods, you're a woman.'

'You can't have a baby unless you're married,' Dorothy said.

'Yes you *can*. Being married's got nothing to do with it. Dot, do calm down, you ought to know all this.'

'Why? I don't believe it. Mumsy would have told me.'

'If she hasn't she probably doesn't know how to. I bet she'll be glad you know already when the time comes.'

'If I tell her you told me she probably won't let me go round with you any more. She'll tell Miss Williams. You could be expelled.'

'Why? Look, I told you, this happens to all of us, all women. Don't you want to know?'

Trying to sound like Stella, trying to remember the right words, Peggy explained everything: periods, eggs, sperm, how to get a baby, how not to get a baby. Dorothy sat as though impaled, fists clenching the bedclothes, elegant legs corkscrewed round each other from the knees down. Peggy's diagram, sketched hastily on the back of the nearest exercise book and looking more like a blueprint for a hot-water system than human female reproductive organs, was at least giving Dorothy some idea of how she functioned inside. When she finally looked up she saw that Dorothy was in tears, silent, agonized tears.

29

'Dot, why's it so awful?'

'It *is* awful,' Dorothy hissed. Her teeth were clenched too. 'It's horrible and disgusting and dirty. And Mumsy said it was all beautiful and sacred.'

'Sacred?'

'Matrimony is a holy estate. It says so in the Book of Common Prayer. She said when I was older I'd understand.'

'Well, you are older and now you do understand,' Peggy said. Oh, to hell with all those useless books and magazines that told you how to get rid of grass stains or embroider dainty handkerchief sachets, where girls never quarrelled over more than misunderstandings or hockey matches. In the old stories they kissed and made up and vowed undying affection. In the modern ones they shook hands with breezy declarations of hatchet-burying and went out to save someone from drowning. Never, never did they fall out because one told the other something really important, something true and, now she thought about it, something so terribly ordinary, which had produced every baby ever born, right back to Cain and Abel.

Dorothy continued to weep silently.

'Do you want a drink of water? An aspirin?' She was beginning to feel panicky herself. The day was ruined, she had ruined it. They had been going to visit the Electric Palace and see a film.

'I want to go home.'

'Well, at least go and wash your face, first.' That's what they always said in those fictional studies and dormitories. *Go and wash your face before tea . . . before prep . . . before*

30

Matron sees you. Dorothy looked beyond face-washing. The silent weeping had become deep whooping sobs.

'*Why* are you so upset?' Peggy persisted. 'I wasn't upset when Stella told me.' She tried to remember how she had felt. 'I was a bit surprised, you know, because I hadn't even begun to guess, but I was awfully interested. I mean, it's science, in a way, isn't it? Think of it as science. Like – like electricity, how a light bulb works. Do you know how a light bulb works? I don't.'

Dorothy got up from the bed and staggered out of the room towards the lavatory, closing the door. Peggy heard the lid of the seat go up. Was Dot going to be sick? Then there was a long silence. Peggy knew she was sitting there, just as she had done once, suddenly aware of everything that was going on inside. She felt sick herself, and guilty, but how could she have known how Dot would take it, Dot so worldly and well-groomed, who talked knowingly, as they all did, of what men were like.

Well, she hadn't known what men were like, or women. Why hadn't someone told her before Peggy had to do it? For the same reason that Hilda had had fits when she found out and had never passed on the knowledge to Peggy. A decent sister would have done that. At least she had Stella, lovely, kind, sensible, honest Stella. She longed for Saturday, when Stella and Irene would bowl up from the station and Peggy could confide in Stella what she had done.

The lavatory cistern flushed. The hand-basin taps ran in the bathroom. There were splashing sounds, Dorothy at last washing her face. When she heard the door open Peggy went to meet her.

'Shall I make some tea?'

'I'm going home,' Dorothy said. In her mind Peggy saw a circle of stones with one in the middle, the Scouts' sign at the end of a trail: I HAVE GONE HOME; so final and always, it seemed to Peggy, a little sad.

'Shall I walk with you? You still look a bit seedy.'

'No,' Dorothy said. 'I don't want Mumsy to see you. She never really liked me being friends with you, she always said . . .'

'Said what?'

But Dorothy was on her way downstairs, head drooping. Peggy stood at the top and watched her go, plucking her hat from the hall stand and letting herself out of the front door.

Chapter 3

She woke next morning with a heavy sense of guilt. She had not felt like that since she was quite small and had done something that Nana had considered a wicked shame. Peggy could rarely see what was so wickedly shameful about what she had done and she could not see it now.

Why should she feel guilty, especially as the whole thing had been an accident? What she had wanted to tell Dorothy about was something quite different and she had havered and delayed because she did not know how to introduce the subject. She might never get the chance now and, in retrospect, Dorothy might not have been the ideal person to tell. She might have taken it quite the wrong way.

For four nights now she had heard the Morse signals. They would begin quite suddenly, go on and on and then stop abruptly; then there might be another burst. They were never loud but they were clear. She could not tell where they were coming from – they were in her head, somewhere, and there was no way of stopping them. They never seemed to come during the day time but, she was beginning to realize, if they did she was unlikely to notice them. Night was silent. A car might pass in the street, a late train go by, but at night, in between those sounds, silence was silent. In the day time, what seemed like silence never was. There was always noise somewhere, voices, gramophones, traffic, perhaps a distant aeroplane, birds singing. Even when there was no definite identifiable sound, daylight murmured.

Last night, when the Morse stopped, had come the strangest thing of all. She could have sworn she heard a voice, tiny, tinny, almost like a miniature telephone, only a few words too indistinct to make out, but a human voice, speaking.

People who heard voices were mad, had to be put away. Relatives mentioned them in hushed tones or not at all; inquiries as to their health were made in very roundabout ways. But people like that didn't just hear voices, they heard voices that told them what to do, and the trouble began when they started to carry out the instructions. Joan of Arc had heard voices and she ended up accused of witchcraft, burned at the stake, although she had insisted that what she had heard were saints, Michael, Margaret and Catherine, speaking to her. And the year before last the Pope had decided, five hundred years after Joan was burned, that she had been telling the truth all along, and made her a saint too.

Peggy did not suppose that Saints Michael, Margaret and Catherine were sending her messages; if they were they'd make sure that she could hear them clearly; after all, they'd been clear enough about telling Joan to lead an army and drive the English out of France. They certainly wouldn't be using Morse code.

* * *

War drums sounded overhead, or Zulus beating their shields; Ollie was at home. Peggy climbed the attic stairs, lit by the tiny window at the bend, and faced the notices on Ollie's door. There was a new one, lettered on a piece of lampshade parchment and singed at the edges. BLAST THY BONES FOUL FIEND AND DAMN THY SOUL WHO ENTERS SIR OLIVER'S DOMAIN. Zulus were out. Ollie had discovered the Middle Ages.

Doubting that Sir Robert Baden Powell would approve of this Scout's address to his fellow man, she knocked on the door. The thumping stopped and Ollie yelled, 'Give the password!'

Peggy put her lips to the keyhole and groaned, 'Excalibur.' This was unlikely to be the password but curiosity and the necessity to repel boarders brought Ollie to the door at once, clutching a home-made longbow.

'What do you want?' he demanded, as disappointed to see her as if he really had expected caitiff knights on the stairs.

'I wanted to ask your advice,' Peggy said.

Few people asked Ollie for advice. He became instantly friendly and slightly condescending. 'How can I help?'

'Do you know all the Morse code?'

'Of course.' But he had to say that.

'No, really *know* it, numbers and everything.' That let him out of feeling that he'd told a lie, if he had paused to think any such thing.

'There's a few I'm not sure of . . .'

'But have you got it written down anywhere. Is there a book?'

'Ye-e-es.' Ollie was looking quizzical and still holding the door half shut. 'Why do you want to know?'

'Why shouldn't I?'

'Girls don't.'

'Girl Guides do, I bet.'

'You're not a Girl Guide.'

'No, but women work the telegraph offices, don't they? There's probably more women than men know Morse.'

Tactless, but Ollie let it pass. 'Do you want to send telegrams, then? Without going to the post office? I say, that would be fraud, wouldn't it?' He began to look interested. 'Where would you get a transmitter? Would you hook up to the lines at the end of the garden?'

Oh, why hadn't she just ransacked his room while she was cleaning it? He'd never have noticed, it always looked ransacked anyway. 'It's just something I'm interested in. I know four letters: O, T, E, A. I want to learn the rest.'

'*Why?*'

He thought she was flying in the face of nature, taxing her delicate feminine brains. She wanted to snap at him, *Why not?* and box his ears. Neither would get her what she was after.

'Why are *you* interested in it, Ollie? Why are you interested in Zulus and – and – tracking and railways and curses?' She tapped the warning on the door.

'I just am.'

'Well, I'm just interested in Morse code. Be a good Scout and lend me yours.'

He closed the door – she could hear him scavenging in a drawer – and returned with a strip of card, the code

36

printed on it. She only then realized that she could have saved herself a lot of trouble by going out and buying one for herself.

'Don't hang on to it,' he said. 'I might need it.'

'I'll copy it out now,' Peggy said. 'You learn things faster if you write them down – oh, and I should get that damn and blast off the door before Hilda sees it.'

'Damn and blast are in Shakespeare.'

'So is murdering little boys,' Peggy said, the code safely in her hand, and skipped downstairs again. From the tiny window at the turn she could see down into the railway cutting, over the fence. From this angle she could also see the wires, carried on posts alongside the track, slung between grids of insulators; the telegraph lines silently bearing coded messages all over the country. What she heard in her head at night was almost as if those messages were somehow leaking out of the wires. Ollie had once remarked on how, if you leaned your ear against a telegraph pole, you could hear it humming.

Humming was not the same as high-speed Morse transmission, humming was musical, and that was the most annoying part of it. When the Morse started up she could not imagine her music. A phantom orchestra in her head was one thing, but a phantom telegraphist . . . ?

Could those telegraph wires be responsible? But you didn't necessarily need wires. She had heard people talk of wire*less* telegraphy. How did that work? Why didn't they learn about it at school? Why did she just have Hilda and Ollie instead of an elder brother who would know about things like this? Vera Openshaw's brother had a motorbike and Vera, it was reputed, had been seen roaring around the country lanes on the pillion. Vera had known how to repair it, too. But the Openshaws were different.

I should have been an Openshaw, Peggy thought, glumly. The Openshaws still had their father.

She sat at her window with the card on the table in front of her and looked at the code. Three dots, S; three dashes, O. Three dots again, S. By holding a pencil upright and keeping her wrist on the table she could produce a convincing rat-a-tat-tat, although nowhere near as fast as the phantom telegraphist. Whoever it was, they knew the code as well as they knew the alphabet; they couldn't possibly be reading off a card as they went, they must be able to *think* in Morse, a whole new language.

Peggy had enough trouble with French, and had not Mlle Chardin said exactly the same thing; not to Peggy but to Edith Rowland, who spoke it beautifully. 'It is not enough to speak beautifully. If you wish to read and speak easily you must learn to *think* in French. While you have to translate every word you will make no progress.' She said something very rapidly in French to Edith, who blinked and floundered. 'You see? How will you dare to have conversations, no matter how well you sound, if you cannot understand?'

'Spiteful old cat,' Edith muttered afterwards, having come up through the school, like everyone else, believing that a beautiful accent was all that mattered, as if they were ever going to *need* the silly language. Mlle Chardin was not old in fact, or a cat. Kind, and a good teacher, she spoke with almost no accent at all and evidently she thought in

English as she wanted them to think in French, although Peggy would have hated to have to parse one of Mademoiselle's sentences. There were so many clauses in them.

Suddenly, thinking in French seemed as easy as pie compared to thinking in Morse. In the Upper VIth you could start learning Greek if you wanted to try for Oxford or Cambridge. Peggy had seen the books in the school library, another new alphabet, but at least in Greek the letters *were* letters. In Morse the letters were made up of dots and dashes; you would have to learn how to make a letter before you could make a word.

But people did, the women who sent and received the messages that were even now passing back and forth along those wires beside the railway line. A couplet of verse came into her head:

Across the wires the electric message came:
'He is no better, he is much the same.'

They had learned that too, at school, as an awful warning on how not to write poetry.

Electric messages; telephones were electric, somewhere along the line. Several houses in the street had telephones – there was a pole just outside the gate. Could she be picking up telephone messages? Stella and Irene had a telephone. The Huttons would have had one too if they could have afforded it as well as Mrs Hendry, but asked if she would prefer a telephone or doing all the cleaning, and the laundry on Mondays, she knew what the answer would be. Anyway, she liked Mrs Hendry, who was downstairs now, finishing off her morning stint. Peggy decided to go down for a chat; her own tappings were becoming almost as much of a distraction as the ones she heard at night.

There was a postcard on the console-table part of the hall stand, posted in Central London late last night. Peggy saw the vision of her flat again for a moment: autumn, a rainy night, flinging on a wrap and running to the pillar box at the corner on a last-minute whim. The card was from Stella, although she must have been in the West End to have got that frank on the stamp; the vision acquired another dimension, going to the theatre on a last-minute whim, because it was there, on the doorstep almost, a dozen, twenty, thirty theatres, concert halls, galleries, exhibitions, museums, picture palaces . . .

Expect us soonest Saturday. 10.30 train, Stella had written as if it really were a telegram she was sending. The postcard was a tinted photograph of Mary Pickford as Little Lord Fauntleroy. Stella must have chosen it for Hilda, who adored Mary Pickford and had several pictures of the actress on her bedroom wall. Peggy and Ollie preferred Buster Keaton, Ollie because Buster could make him fall off his seat laughing. Peggy laughed too but secretly thought that without the make-up that film actors had to wear, he must be a very good-looking man. That really did have to be kept a secret, fancying Buster Keaton when the rest of the school was in love with Douglas Fairbanks.

She left the card on the hall stand and went along to the kitchen, where Mrs Hendry was mopping the floor having cleaned out the coke boiler and laid it ready for lighting later; bath night.

'Mind your feet, Miss— Oh, it's you, Peg. Hop up on the table if you're staying.'

Peggy found herself a niche between two upended chairs and sat, feet dangling, while Mrs Hendry finished off. Mrs Hendry knew that Hilda would be affronted if she addressed her as anything but Miss Hilda, and that Peggy would be equally embarrassed if she called her Miss Peggy except when Hilda was around to overhear. Ollie was supposed to be Master Ollie.

'You might as well call me Miss Margaret,' Peggy had said once, when they were sharing a mid-morning bun and a cup of tea, 'if we're going to be *that* la-di-da.'

She did wonder sometimes what would happen if Hilda met Maurice Hendry, who was at the grammar school on a scholarship. Would she expect *him* to call her Miss Hilda; would he do it? There were five young Hendrys: Mavis, a year older than Peggy, worked in Lipton's. David, named after Lloyd George, was about to follow his brother to King Edward's and Ollie would be joining them. Nancy and Iris were still at the elementary. Peggy had gathered from their mother's remarks that if the High School offered scholarships all the Hendrys would be getting educated above themselves, as Dorothy's mother would have put it. Probably Hilda agreed. How awful, Hilda would think, to find yourself sharing a form room, playing hockey, singing in the choir with your charwoman's daughter. But Peggy had seen Nancy and Iris; they looked like fun. Mavis often served her when she went shopping. She had had her blond hair bobbed and it fluffed up like swan's down on either side of her face, fair and feathery. She had not met Maurice but she imagined that he looked like Buster Keaton.

'Stella's coming tomorrow,' Peggy said.

'You're telling me,' Mrs Hendry remarked. 'I've been making up the spare beds. When your mum gets in tell her that last sheet's going home. I don't think it'll stand another wash.'

'Sides to middle again,' Peggy sighed. 'That'll be me.' They divided the mending between them. Hilda, who darned exquisitely, took care of socks and stockings and elbows, which was fine by Peggy. Ollie went through at least three or four heels a week. Peggy saw to the linen and towels, dull but straightforward, hems and seams. But a bed sheet was Purgatory, cutting it down the middle, so that the worn patch went to the sides, then stitching the selvedges together and sewing new side hems. Straightforward it might be, but surrounded by the heavy unwieldy folds of sheeting she found it difficult to keep the seams straight and flat on the sewing machine with one hand while turning the handle with the other. Peggy's seams had lumps and strange curves in them. She spent as much time unpicking as sewing. Dorothy's mother had a treadle machine but she was not the one who used it. Someone came in once a week to do the mending and Peggy doubted if any sheets were turned sides to middle in the Prior household.

Mrs Hendry could always spot Peggy's handiwork in the laundry. 'You ought to take more care with your tacking,' she said. 'It doesn't take all that long. I bet you try and save time by doing it with the pins in.'

Peggy nodded sheepishly.

'You'll never get it flat like that. Pin it, tack it – one-inch stitches – take the pins out, iron the seam and there you go. Didn't your mum show you how?'

'It's all such a fag,' Peggy said.

'Yes, but think how much time you'd save not unpicking it.'

'That's true. I just hate sewing. Buttonholes are the worst. When I was in the Upper Third I had to spend two whole terms doing buttonholes in needlework, nothing but buttonholes, and when I went up I was still so bad I had to do them again. I wish someone would invent something that went down both sides of your blouse or coat and when you put them together they just joined up.'

'Funny you should say that.' Mrs Hendry was wringing out the mop in the scullery. 'Maurice was telling me only the other day, there's some foreign thing, Swedish I think he said, hundreds of little metal teeth – just like you were saying – down two bits of cloth, and a sort of tag at the bottom, and when you pull it all the teeth can hook together.'

'Why can't we buy them if someone's invented them?' Peggy complained.

'Probably because they're foreign. People don't trust them.'

'Why, in case they bite? Do you know, Hilda told me, when the war started a whole lot of girls in the upper school got together and said they wouldn't play music by

43

Germans, and the mistresses agreed, can you believe it? So for four years nobody played any Bach or Beethoven or Mendelssohn or Brahms – I mean, how *barmy*. There was hardly anyone left worth playing, as if Brahms had anything to do with invading Belgium.'

Trust Maurice to have known about the magic fastener, though.

'Mrs Hendry, does Maurice understand about electricity, telegraph, things like that?'

'Wouldn't put it past him. There's not much he doesn't know about, he was born curious. I can't remember when he wasn't asking questions – like you, now I come to think of it.'

'Would he know about wireless telegraphy, do you think?'

'It's wireless telephony now, radio he calls it, all that Marconi business. He's been working down the Co-op all through the holidays saving up for a receiving set; gave half his earnings to me, kept the other half for this receiver. He says we'll all be picking it up soon.'

Not only did Maurice know about wireless communication, so did his mother, by the sound of it.

'A receiving set?'

'For the broadcasting, to pick up music and things. He showed me a picture. Why they call it wireless I can't imagine, there's wires all over the shop. And you have to plug it in, for which you need electricity, which we have not got. I think he wants to take it to school.'

We've got electricity, Peggy thought, and imagined, when she had worked out the scenario, inviting Maurice

Hendry to bring his receiving set round to the house to plug it in and . . . receive, whatever it was you received. Radio, of course; that was how they had caught the notorious Dr Crippen, fleeing to America on an ocean liner. There were no telegraph wires to a ship – so that must be the other way, wireless telegraphy, radio. She was always seeing pieces about it in the paper, but no one ever explained what it was, how it worked, and since it was something they could not afford she never took much notice. But perhaps it was not all that expensive, if Maurice Hendry was getting it. So stupid, all those chances to find out passed up. But could anyone explain how you might pick up radio *without* a receiving set?

Chapter 4

Peggy went down to the station to meet Stella and Irene. She did the weekend shopping first and the basket was heavy. A wicker twig had worked loose at the bottom and snagged her stocking when she picked it up. She would have preferred a big roomy bag made of American cloth like Mrs Hendry's, but Hilda thought that would look low. Peggy thought that you couldn't get any lower than calling something low – still, serve Hilda right; she would have to mend the stocking.

It was one of their minor economies, hauling home the groceries instead of having them sent. If they shopped at the Co-op it would have been Maurice perhaps who would have delivered them and she could have asked him about radio.

Outside the draper's she ran into Daphne Roper. Peggy, Daphne, Dorothy and Olive Stapleton made up a casual quartet at school and often met in the holidays. Daphne looked askance at the basket – her people had their groceries delivered – but said nothing about Dorothy. So Dorothy herself had said nothing. What could she have said? But when term began something would have to happen.

Daphne was matching embroidery silks for her mother and invited Peggy to help, making it sound like a thrilling adventure requiring virtuoso co-ordination of hand and eye. Peggy had the excuse of the 10.30 train and used it. Talking to Daphne made her feel uncomfortable.

The station platforms were dry and dusty in the sunshine, the enamel signs for Virol and Marmite and Reckitt's Blue radiated heat. It was getting to the stale end of summer where people had given up saying, 'Lovely day,' because everything was looking overcooked and limp, leaves matt, flowers drooping. The Up platform was crowded, people waiting for the cheap excursion train to London; only one or two stood on the Down side, there, as she was, to meet passengers alighting. Tab, the station cat, was spread out in the shade, too hot even to go after the station sparrows. When the signal dropped with a clunk, up by the bridge, he flicked an ear and closed his eyes again, not bothering to look when the engine wheezed into sight. Usually he sprang up and advanced stiff-legged to the gate, where people would pause to give up their tickets and had a moment to pass the time of day with him.

Irene and Stella were in the end carriage and stepped down almost before the train had squealed to a halt, carrying little cases and light linen coats, looking like two schoolgirls in their summer dresses; schoolgirls out of a book. Real schoolgirls never looked like that, as Peggy knew only too well. Both of them had bobbed hair, Stella's straight and dark, Irene's fair and curly. Peggy yearned to bob her hair. 'Do you want to look like a factory girl?' Hilda had said. 'No, I want to look like Aunt Stella,' Peggy had retorted. 'You'll be asking to paint your face, next,' Hilda jeered. Mother had just said feebly, 'Not yet, darling.

47

When I was your age I couldn't wait to put my hair up.'

Nobody put their hair up any more, surely, not when they were young, except prefects, who did strange folds and tucks with their plaits to disguise the fact that they still had long hair. She sometimes despaired of Mother, who had done war work and was now the family breadwinner with her job at the library, too timid to tell Hilda to mind her own business; Hilda, her eldest child to be sure, but still only her child. Hilda had far too much to say in the running of the household, in Peggy's opinion. She always had had a say, since they moved from Bedford Avenue to Gladstone Road, but it was only recently that she had started saying it.

'Here's lovely Peg, come to meet us,' Irene said, clapping her on the shoulder. Stella and Irene were not the kissing kind. 'Oh, look at all that shopping. What a marvellous excuse – let's take a cab.'

'Much too hot to walk,' Stella said. 'You haven't got any ice in that basket, have you?'

'No, why?'

'We've brought raspberries and cream. Let's stop at MacFisheries and buy a block, I've got a wonderful recipe for iced cream pudding. Is Ollie at home?'

'I shouldn't think so.'

'Pity, he could have been usefully employed smashing up the ice. Oh well, we'll do it ourselves. Does that lazy little toad do anything around the house?'

'No, he's a Scout now. He has to go out and find good deeds to do.'

'All I've ever seen him find is golf balls,' Stella said.

Irene snorted. 'You've got to get him trained, Peg. Think ahead. What's he going to be like in ten years' time? He won't be doing good deeds then, I'll bet, he'll be just like every other young man, unable to stir a step without half a dozen women in the background to keep him going. He's nearly four years younger than you, but he'll be able to vote before you can. Ask yourself, do you want the country run by people like Ollie?'

'It already is,' Stella said. 'They don't improve with age. Calm down, Reenie, you're not on the stump now.'

They piled into a taxi.

'What's the stump?'

'Electioneering. One woman in Parliament's not enough.'

'Are you standing for Parliament?' Peggy said. Parliament was men in top hats and watch chains. What would they do when Irene bounded in among them?

'She isn't. We're mobilizing a candidate. Reenie, no politics this weekend, please.'

At the fishmonger's the cab stopped and Irene went to buy the ice. Peggy saw the sun gleam malevolently on MacMorris's brass plate, next door.

'How's things?' Stella asked, while they were alone. 'You look rather down.'

'Oh, just the usual ructions with Hilda,' Peggy said. It was no time for confidences, there were only two or three people in the fish shop. If she had a chance later she would get Stella alone and tell her about the awful scene with Dorothy. 'I say, if I got my hair bobbed you'd back me up, wouldn't you? And I had a tooth filled on Monday, it still aches.'

'It ought to have settled down by now,' Stella said. 'Don't suffer in silence, go back and have it seen to. What does that have to do with getting your hair bobbed? Oh, here comes the ice.'

Irene climbed back in with a small iceberg wrapped in paper. 'Top speed, now,' she said to the driver, 'or we'll have a lake in here.'

The house came to life with Stella in it. Ollie, who had made the mistake of slipping home for a moment to collect provisions, was sent outside with the coal hammer to break up the ice. Irene hulled the raspberries and strained them while Stella made coffee. Mother sat by protesting ineffectually.

'I can't have you coming here and doing all the work.'

'Rubbish. Ollie's doing the hard labour – which is good for his soul. Is there a cucumber in the house? We can do tea in style – cucumber sandwiches and raspberry cream ice. Get the smallest cake tin, Peg; we can freeze it in that, put the ice in a bucket and the cake tin in the ice. Where's the coolest spot, the larder? Someone will have to remember to stir it every hour on the hour or we'll end up with a solid block and have to smash that with the coal hammer.'

Hilda kept very quiet. Nose out of joint, Peggy thought. Hilda was the one who gave orders. Perhaps she did not entirely approve of Stella and Irene; she never spoke of them with any warmth or seemed to look forward to their visits. It was different when Stella came alone. It was Stella-and-Irene who made her so silent and wary. Why?

They were both such fun and how could anyone be anything but pleasantly envious of the way they lived in their flat, doing jobs they enjoyed, entertaining themselves as they pleased? As far as Peggy could see, the only thing they ever did that displeased them was going to church with the family on Sunday mornings.

'Don't you go in London?' Peggy had asked once, after Irene had let something slip.

'Oh, sometimes to sung evensong at one of the big churches; the music can be heavenly and there's no sermon.'

'That's not really going to church, is it?'

'No,' Stella had said, frankly. 'We don't "go to church". Have you thought of what the Church says about women? If Joan of Arc had been a man they'd have agreed her voices came from God and made her a saint on the spot. We go with you when we're here to keep Mary happy.'

Not that they always stuck to that. One or other would develop a convenient headache or neuralgia after breakfast on Sunday although never, by a kind of gentlemanly agreement, both at the same time.

This Sunday Peggy had hoped devoutly, although she had not the cheek to pray for it, that they would be feeling equally healthy so that she could have a pain of her own. She did not want to go to church, to sit in the usual pew, which was just across the aisle from the one where the Priors sat. There had been no word from Dorothy; better still, no word from Mrs Prior to Mother, but what would happen when she smiled across the aisle to Dorothy as usual, when Mother and Mrs Prior exchanged greetings or

51

chatted in the churchyard afterwards as they so often did?

Coward, she told herself. Face it out, see it through. They can't shoot you.

But if it all came out, Mother's wounded look and Hilda's outraged nagging would be as bad as bullets.

God, however, as he was supposed to be able to do, knew her inmost thought without her having to say anything. By the time breakfast was over her jaw was aching again. Before Stella or Irene had a chance to offer an excuse she had a real one of her own. Stella noticed.

'Tooth still playing up?' she inquired casually.

Peggy nodded. 'It's been aching a bit since the raspberry cream last night. It was glorious, but so cold.'

'She can't go to church with toothache, Mary,' Stella said.

'Considering what so many men have suffered I would have thought you could at least try to put up with it,' Hilda said. 'Clove oil.'

'Don't be so heartless.' Irene said it lightly but Hilda flushed. 'Or so pi,' she added under her breath. 'You try sitting through matins with toothache. It's the worst pain there is – you sit there thinking, I'd rather have my head cut off.'

'You'd better take aspirin and oil of cloves and go and lie down, darling,' Mother said. 'You really will have to go back to Mr MacMorris if it doesn't get better soon.'

Sunday silence was more silent than weekday silence, once the church bells had stopped clamouring. Peggy lay on the couch in the parlour with a magazine that Irene had thoughtfully left for her, but it was floppy and difficult to handle lying down. In the end she let it drop, closed her eyes ... and immediately the Morse code started up, *ditditdit-dit-dit-dit-ditditditdit-dit*. She bore it for ten minutes, hoping it would stop again, but on it went, and on and on. It was worse than the toothache because she could get at that, rub it, anoint it with oil, but there was no way she could get at the Morse.

At last she got up, crossed the room and wound up the gramophone. If the Morse had driven the music from her head at least she could drive away the Morse with music. She put a ragtime record on the turntable. It was not Sunday music. She would have to stop before twelve, when they would all be home again.

Ragtime was not good for teeth. If only it weren't so hot. When the record ended she put it away and closed the lid of the gramophone. In the sudden hush she waited for the Morse to reassert itself but instead she heard the sound that might be a voice again, high, vibrant, with that strange fuzzy quality of a wasp in a tin can, but before she could be sure of what she was hearing, or thought she was hearing, there was another sound outside in the street: a motorcar.

She went to the bay window and looked out, kneeling on the couch. No one in Gladstone Road owned a car and on the whole they did not know the kind of people who would own cars. Her own arrival yesterday in a cab, with Stella and Irene, had produced curious looks. The neighbours rarely used cabs, either.

It was an open car, low slung, sporty, painted a glossy maroon with much brasswork, and built for speed, but it was moving very slowly, coming to a halt. Both the driver, a young man, and a boy in the passenger seat, were peering and pointing at something – numbers on gates. They had stopped right outside the house. The boy vaulted out without bothering to open the door, and put his hand on the gate. The driver called him back and they both laughed. The driver descended and walked round the front of the car, pausing to admire it as if he hadn't had it very long.

They both came up the path. The boy saw Peggy at the window and waved and Peggy, who had forgotten that they could see her as well as she could see them, waved back guiltily. Hilda would have something to say about people who gaped out of windows like housemaids, but better to gape in plain sight than lurk behind lace curtains like the people opposite.

There was a knock at the door. Probably they assumed that she would not be answering it herself, expecting one of those maids to appear. Who could they be? As she went into the hall she noticed that she had creased her frock horribly again, lying on the couch; why couldn't someone invent a cloth that didn't wrinkle if you so much looked at it? No one would mistake *her* for a maid in a neat black dress and starched apron.

When she opened the door they were standing in the porch and swept off their caps together. They were very alike, the boy only a little shorter than the man and both very like someone else, although for a moment she could not think who it was.

The man said, 'Good morning, is Miss Summersby at home?'

They'd got the wrong house. Peggy's disappointment was so great that she only then knew how pleased she had been at the prospect of interesting visitors.

'Miss Summersby doesn't— Oh!' She knew who they looked like. 'You mean Irene.' No one ever thought of her as Miss Summersby.

'Rather; our sister,' the boy said. 'He's Ted, I'm Brian.'

'Sorry to bother you,' Ted said, quelling his brother with an elbow. 'We motored to Town to see Irene on the off-chance, and the neighbours rather thought she and Stella might be here.'

'They are – only they aren't. I mean, they've gone to church. They won't be long, do come in.'

What a good thing it was Sunday and the house was tidy. She did not have to do a lightning calculation about which room they could safely be shown into, although the parlour must smell dreadfully of cloves. She paused at the sitting-room door. How strange, her tooth had quite stopped hurting.

'Can I get you some coffee?'

'Would you mind if we had something cold? It's hotter than Hades out there,' Ted said.

'I say, ladies present. You're not in the mess now,' Brian said.

'We didn't call it Hades in the mess,' Ted said.

He'd been a soldier. Did he want beer? Brandy and soda? What did men drink? 'We've got lemonade.'

'Splendid. I say, don't feel you've got to wait on us. Let's come and get it.'

They followed her into the kitchen. What a shame all

the ice had melted. Cold lemonade would be much nicer than tepid lemonade, and more hospitable.

'You must think we're the most awful oafs,' Ted apologized. 'We barge in on you, no proper introductions—'

'That's right. Actually we are burglars but we prefer to do things the easy way. Such a bore, climbing drainpipes. Now, hapless female, give us your valuables.'

'Shut up,' Ted said, raising his elbow again. 'Don't say things like that, it could be only too true. We really are Irene's brothers. We know the address because she's sent postcards from here, but I'm terribly sorry, we don't know who you are. One of the Miss Holts?'

'Stella's my aunt. We're Huttons. I'm Peggy.'

'We'd better shake hands,' Brian said, 'now we've got that straightened out. How do you do, Miss Peggy Hutton. Are there any more at home like you?'

'There's Mother, and Hilda and Ollie, and no one's home, I told you,' Peggy said.

'No mad wife in the attic?'

'*Will* you stow it?' Ted said. 'Look, I know you're our hostess and all that but why don't we go and sit in the garden – I say! Open country.' He was leaning out of the window, which from his angle gave a misleading view. 'You'd never expect that after all those little streets.'

They would have to go out through the scullery unless she herded them back into the sitting room and through the French windows, but they hardly seemed the types to care. Peggy led the way down the path to the quince tree, where there was a wooden bench seat, but Ted and Brian sat down on the grass.

It was all very rustic. She would have to confess before a train came through and ruined the idyll. 'It's not all that open, actually. That's the golf links across there, but there's a railway just over the fence, in a cutting.'

Brian immediately got up to look. 'Aren't you lucky. Is this the main line? You must see some stunning engines.'

'No, it's not. We don't. The really annoying thing is having to go down to the station to catch the trains. It would be so handy if we could just hail them like cabs when we wanted to get on. They're very slow just here.'

The conversation flagged again.

'Fine quinces,' Ted said.

'Do you play golf?' Brian asked.

Golf? With the price of club membership? They could barely afford the occasional game of tennis at the courts in the park. Did people like this with beautiful motorcars understand about money? She knew, painfully, that the only people who talked about money were the ones who didn't have any. School had taught her that. It was going to be embarrassing for Mother when they came back from church and she would have to ask them to stay to lunch out of politeness. But they were so nice. She must warn them herself, now, because although lunch was cold meat and salad there was just enough for six. It would stretch, but only if everything were rationed out, one cut, one tomato, a couple of lettuce leaves, three radishes and a bit of beet-root, cucumber – there was still a half left over from yesterday, Hilda had sliced it so thinly. Or she might toss the salad – but there would still be nothing left in the bowl after one serving.

And where would they all sit? They couldn't be invited to pig it in the kitchen but would the table in the sitting room, which doubled as a dining room, seat eight? There was only one leaf in it; Ollie was using the other as a shelf, or a ski slope or something. She could hardly say, 'Were you hoping to be asked to stay to lunch because you'll wish you hadn't.' If she trimmed the fat off the mutton it would look even smaller, and there was scarcely any lemonade left – and only one lemon—

Whatever she said she was going to be in for it with Mother and Hilda, who would be humiliated, not because they were running out of food but because people would know they hadn't much money. As if anyone could fail to notice, Peggy thought. They'd only have to look at *her*. She tried to tuck the gym shoes out of sight and plunged in, 'Would you care to stay to lunch?' That sounded nicely informal. 'It'll be sort of pot luck – we never have much on Sundays, not in summer, just a bit of salad.' Wait till you see that bit.

'Very sensible,' Ted Summersby said. 'Before the war our people used to have a vast Sunday dinner, even on days like this, which was hard on the servants, but they started to feel that they shouldn't indulge when so many were having to go without. Somehow we've never got back into the habit of those huge blow-outs. We wouldn't dream of imposing upon you, Peggy. What we were thinking of was a picnic. The original plan was to pick up the girls in Marylebone and drive out into the country. We rose at dawn. It was going to be a surprise party.'

'We have a hamper,' Brian said.

'It'll still be a surprise,' Peggy said. 'They thought they were going to get cold mutton.'

'But won't you join us?'

Peggy's mind was on rationing. 'There's six of us altogether.'

'The hamper's grossly overloaded. You contribute your bit of salad and we'll do fine.'

'I don't suppose everybody will come,' Peggy said. 'But I'd love to and wild horses won't stop Ollie once he's seen your car.'

There were voices in the house. Peggy saw someone opening the French windows – Hilda, who must have seen them in the garden. Hilda would never demean herself before company by coming out through the scullery. Fortunately Stella and Irene were less fussy, already striding towards them over the grass.

'Hi, chaps,' Irene said, casually. 'How did you find us?'

Stella grabbed the last of the lemonade and said quietly to Peggy, 'Go and find your mother. Something happened.'

'An accident?'

'No, no. Not bloodshed. One of your friends, I think. She's upset, though. Come and cry on my shoulder later.'

Dorothy! Oh, what had she said, what had Mrs Prior said? The sun was bright, Stella and Irene and the Summersby brothers were laughing and talking and she was in a chill dark place, out of it. She turned away and walked back up the garden into the house, passing Hilda, who was on the way down.

'Who on earth are those people?' Hilda asked, as if

Peggy had been out trawling the streets for derelicts. 'Why did you ask them in?'

'Irene's brothers,' Peggy said. 'I had to do the polite, I was the only one here. I suppose you'd have made them wait in the porch.'

'There's no need to sprawl on the grass like that, and what have you been up to with that Prior girl? Her mother actually cut us.'

'Shouldn't think she even noticed *you*,' Peggy muttered and went indoors.

Ollie was crashing about upstairs, changing out of his Sunday suit and making as much row as if he really were wearing the armour he fancied himself in. Mother was in the kitchen, peering anxiously into the larder.

'It's all right, they aren't here for lunch,' Peggy said.

'Who are they? Peggy, you really shouldn't have asked them in.'

'Ted and Brian Summersby,' Peggy said. 'They came to see Irene and they've brought a picnic. We're all invited.'

Mother looked slightly less distracted, but not cheerful.

'Peggy, darling, the most awkward thing happened in church. The Priors were there, of course, and I thought Dorothy might ask if you were ill, but they didn't even look at us, and after the service I said good morning to Mrs Prior – and she *cut* me. She wouldn't look at me, nor would Dorothy. Have you quarrelled?'

'Sort of,' Peggy said. This was worse than she had feared. If Mrs Prior had complained she could have defended herself, but now she was left with the burden of having to explain. She couldn't, not now, and ruin everyone's lovely day by bringing a cloud of disapproval down on them all, especially with two strange young men there.

'What do you mean, sort of? I wish you wouldn't be so slangy. What did you quarrel about? Why is Mrs Prior so offended?'

'It was — is — private, something I said to Dorothy that she didn't like.' That was true enough. 'Nothing to do with her mother. I think Mrs Prior was very rude to cut you — and very silly.'

'Peggy! That's enough.' It was not done to tell one adult that another was silly, even if they'd said it first.

'Well, it doesn't really matter, does it? She's not your friend, Mrs Prior's not.'

'That's got nothing to do with it. She may say . . . something, to other people. And what will happen if she comes into the library?'

'She won't,' Peggy said. 'She doesn't use the public library because she's afraid of catching germs from books. You know, *common* people use it. She'd rather pay sixpence a go from Mudie's Circulating. I told Dorothy I was surprised she didn't think *I'd* spread infection that I'd picked up from a library book.'

'Is that what you quarrelled about?'

It hadn't been but on an earlier occasion they had had words about it, forgotten as soon as Dorothy, with a little prodding from Peggy, remembered that Mrs Hutton was a brave war widow. Being a brave war widow would not heal the breach this time.

Before Peggy could frame an answer everyone came in from the garden and Ollie avalanched downstairs in case he was missing something. Irene introduced her brothers and hands were shaken.

'Will you join us, Mrs Hutton?' Ted said, winningly. 'If you don't mind us requisitioning your salad.'

'We can't all get in the Morris,' Brian said. 'Shall we hire a cab and form a convoy?'

'I could stand on the running board,' Ollie said, imagining the car packed and toppling with Keystone Kops.

The kitchen was far too small for eight people. Peggy wondered vaguely how the occupants had managed when the house was first built and they had all been wearing bustles.

When they had sorted themselves out Mother decided to stay at home and Hilda said she couldn't possibly leave her, as though Mother were delicate and unable to move without assistance. Peggy thought that in her place she would have been glad to see the back of them all. Hilda made further pointed remarks about people whose toothache miraculously disappeared although it had been so bad that they had had to miss matins.

As the Summersbys had provisioned themselves so generously the Huttons had only to contribute a few apples and two of the tomatoes. Then they all crammed into the Morris, which Ollie had been adoring in the street, while the girls got ready. Brian swung the handle, the engine turned and coughed as he climbed into the back. Irene was sitting at the front with Ted, Stella and Peggy took the rear seats while the boys perched on the folded-down hood.

The motor was too noisy for much conversation. Stella shouted directions over Ted's shoulder, Brian and Ollie flourished their caps in lordly fashion to passing pedestrians. Brian must be nearer to Hilda's age than Ollie's, but they had hit it off immediately. Peggy was so glad that Hilda had stopped at home. She would have said that they looked like a charabanc outing and had Ollie down from his perch because he was lowering the tone. But if you couldn't let rip in a car like this, where could you? It might be ages before they got another chance.

Chapter 5

They drove into open country, past the last of the new villas that were creeping among the fields, and started to look out for likely places to stop and picnic.

'We need a tree,' Irene said, 'for shade.'

'And somewhere to play cricket,' Brian commanded, 'and a pub. We might run out of drink.'

A pub! Hilda would die of mortification.

'Don't look so shocked,' Stella said. 'Village inns are nothing like your corner boozer. Anyway the boys can bring out jugs. You needn't set your maidenly foot inside.'

'I shouldn't care,' Peggy said. 'I was thinking of Hilda.'

'Hilda would picket the door with a banner,' Irene said, 'and sing, "For Mother's sake, dear Father, don't touch the demon Drink."'

Brian and Ollie were yelling, 'Stop! There it is! Perfect!'

They had come to a place that had everything – a village green with trees along one side and an inn called the Royal Oak. There was no one about. The pub, the few cottages, the church with its squat Kentish tower looked asleep, like cows lying down in a field. It was as hot as it had been at home but a dozy, gentle kind of heat.

Leaving the car under one tree, where it clicked as it cooled down, they picnicked under another and then

64

played French cricket on the green, one batsman, one bowler and four fielders.

Cricket at school was never much fun, always spoiled by vigorous lectures on team spirit and not letting the side down, however much you felt like a lone hero at the wicket. Here it really was five to one and when you were out you went into the field and ganged up on the next batsman instead of trudging back to the pavilion for yet another diatribe on poor sportsmanship, lack of backbone and feeble excuses. *You're just slacking!*

It was all very leisurely here. A deep fielder who wanted to lie on the grass and nibble daisies was not whipped back into line with strident cries of 'Shirker! I can't *stand* shirkers! Where's your team spirit?'

The second time she was caught out Stella went to sit under the picnic tree near to where Peggy was standing.

'Let the flannelled fools at the wicket have their fun, Peg. Come and chat. Ollie can cover your silly square leg or whatever it is. It's good for him to run about.'

Peggy sat down beside her aunt. In spite of all the exertion Stella looked clean and cool in a blue-and-white striped dress like the Kodak girl. They were all barefoot. Stella waggled her toes.

'Isn't this the best way to spend Sunday? We earned it, anyway, listening to that dreadful old gasbag this morning. "God moves in a mysterious way." If I had a pound for every time I heard that these days, I'd never have to work again. It's the answer to everything, hadn't you noticed? Bad housing, infant mortality, unemployment. "Why did my husband die and leave me with eight kids to feed?"

"Why did my only son die?" "Why did millions die?" "Why did the ones who survived the trenches come home to die of influenza?" "God works in mysterious ways, my child." You did well to miss it, Peg. Was it really toothache or did you know something was going to happen?'

'What did happen?'

'Don't play the innocent babe. That ridiculous woman cutting Mary in church; and her idiot daughter; and her poor fish of a husband who hadn't a clue what was going on and didn't know where to look. That's why Mary was so upset – she didn't know what was going on, either. Come on, kiddo, tell all. You can trust Auntie.'

'It was something I said to Dorothy, and she didn't know what I was talking about and I had to explain. About monthlies. I just told her what you told me, and it was awful. She didn't know *anything*. And she couldn't understand why, so I had to tell her about having babies, too.'

'I bet she didn't know about that, either,' Stella said. 'Where did she think they come from, under gooseberry bushes? Out of flowers? We were told the doctor brought them in his black bag. Oh *dear*. Was she very upset?'

'And frightened. She didn't want to believe me but she could see I wasn't making it up. And she said her mother had told her it was all beautiful and sacred. And now I suppose she's told her mother it's not beautiful and sacred at all.'

'Her mother who looks just like a flat fish? Any flatter and she'd have both eyes on the same side of her head; forceps delivery, I'd guess. She ought to be grateful. If she hadn't told Dorothy herself it was probably because she was too embarrassed. Well, cheer up, Peg. She'll also be too embarrassed to complain about it – she hasn't complained, has she? No pained little notes?'

'She can't have. It was nearly a week ago. Mother would have said. Oh, Stella, there's worse. She was so scared about the baby, growing inside – well, no, at least she knew something about that. It was how it gets born that really upset her, so I had to tell her that you could – that you didn't have to—'

'What? You gave her Marie Stopes as well? Oh, my God.'

'What shall I *do*?'

'Nothing,' Stella said, firmly, 'unless being without Dorothy is breaking your heart. Is she your absolute bestest pal, till death do us part?'

'Not *that* best but – well, yes. I suppose so. We always go around together.'

'Can you live without her? I mean, are you looking so sick – yes, you are, chick – because she won't talk to you or because you're afraid of what will happen?'

Was she missing Dorothy? No, not really. If she could have swapped this happy afternoon for an afternoon with Dorothy she would not have considered it for a moment. If they'd been true friends Dorothy could have gone ahead and been upset without turning against her, because you knew that your real friends would never hurt you for no reason. Dorothy had thought at first that she was lying and afterwards, just being hateful.

'I was afraid of Mother being upset. And if anything gets said at school—'

'Considering it's an all-female establishment you'd think something would get said. Don't you girls ever discuss anything important?'

'I expect the older ones do.' But did they? *Hilda?*

'Look, Peg, I'll talk to Mary when we get home, and I dare say she'll be all floppy and horrified but I won't let her go until I've made her see that you've done your friend a good turn. She'll understand. And if there's one *word* of fuss at school I'll be down from Town on my broomstick to rescue you.'

Stella put her arm around Peggy's shoulder and squeezed it briefly, much more reassuring than hugs and kisses.

'Now, what about that toothache? You weren't inventing it, were you?'

'No, it really did hurt. It's fine though, now – but, Stella, there's something else, something really odd. I've only noticed it since I had the tooth filled, because I've been lying down more, I expect. I can hear things.'

'What sort of things?'

'It sounds like Morse code.'

'Tapping? You're sure it's not the cold water pipes?'

'You know what our water pipes sound like. They grind and clang. You expect something solid to come out of the tap, in lumps. No, this is very high-pitched and fast, incredibly fast.'

'Really skilful telegraphists can transmit up to forty words a minute. Can you make out what it says?'

'No. I've been trying to learn it, but I could never decode at that speed. And once or twice I've thought I heard a voice.'

'What did it say?'

Peggy looked round at Stella to see if she were laughing, but she seemed perfectly serious.

'I couldn't tell that either. It's all buzzy.'

'Where does it come from?'

'It's in my head. I know it's not the water pipes – it isn't coming *from* anywhere, it's just *there*. I'm not imagining it.'

'You could be,' Stella said, thoughtfully, 'even if you didn't think you were. Didn't you tell me once that you could make yourself play music in your head?'

'That's real music, music I know, music *by* people. I'm only remembering it, really, like a gramophone record. I'm not remembering this.'

'I didn't mean that kind of imagining,' Stella said. 'I meant hearing something quite ordinary and fooling yourself into thinking that it was something quite different – no, don't be offended. If you can't tell what a sound is right away you can easily mistake it for something else – or if you don't know how far away it is. I remember once when we took a cottage in the country; I woke up one morning and I thought I heard water pouring onto stone from a height, spattering. I supposed Irene was emptying a jug out of the window, onto flagstones, but it was the farmer in the next field, burning brushwood. Until I saw it I thought flames crackling was the splashing of water. You can't get much more different than that.'

'But those were real sounds,' Peggy said, 'even the one you only thought you heard. But mine are in my head. If I put my fingers in my ears I can still hear them. Do you think I'm going mad?'

'Good heavens, what makes you think you might be?'

'Robert Schumann.'

'Who?'

'The composer. He heard music. At first he thought it was angels singing but in the end he said it sounded like demons in Hell.'

'I never knew that. Talking to you is an education, my girl. If it only comes occasionally it doesn't sound like incipient insanity. How long's it been going on – a week? I'd give it a bit longer, if I were you, and see what happens. It might be tinnitus but I've never heard of that sounding like Morse. Is it happening now?'

'No, only when it's really quiet.'

'If it were a real voice giving you strange messages, that would be different.'

'It's not like that.'

'Well, leave it for a little and don't start worrying about it yet. You may find it goes away on its own. Look, I think this game is winding down – everyone's dropped out except the boys. We ought to be thinking about packing up. Ted will drive Irene and me back to London after we've delivered you and Ollie.'

The day had gone so quickly. Time always did when you were enjoying yourself, but even Brian and Ollie were flagging. Ted and Irene were sitting against the Morris, smoking cigarettes – oh, Hilda! – and the shadows of the trees were creeping across the green.

'It would be lovely to live here, wouldn't it?' Peggy said. 'Those little cottages, that church—'

'Those little cottages are probably damp and leaking,

rats in the thatch, no drains. Being poor in the country is as bad as being poor in town. You don't care about the view and the roses round the door if your children are sick and your man's out of work. There's no gas here, no electricity. I expect the big house has a telephone, if there is a big house, and the vicar. But it's all very well for a visit, we can always come back – if we ever find out what the place is called. Perhaps it's better not to. I read a wonderful book while I was in France, *Le Grand Meaulnes*. It's about a schoolboy, older than you – Brian's age. He gets lost while he's out in the country – he doesn't know where he is, and he comes to a mysterious old manor house where the people are having a wedding party. He joins them, has a strange, wonderful time, meets a girl, falls in love . . . then he comes home. He gets a lift in the dark. He doesn't know where he's been, or how to find the place again. It becomes his dream to return there, to find his girl again.'

'Does he? Does he get back?'

'Yes,' Stella said. 'In the end he does, when he's a man – well, a little older. And ruins everything. He was better off with the dream. The point is, if he'd really put his mind to it he could have found the place at any time, it wasn't that far away, but yearning for it was much more romantic. While he was young enough to enjoy yearning, everything was safe. Don't let's find out what this village is called. Let's just remember a lovely day and long to come back. If we ever do it will be by accident, and that won't spoil the magic.'

'Do you have the book? Could I read it?'

'I borrowed my copy and gave it back, and I don't know

if it's been translated into English. How well do you read French?'

'Well enough for school, but we never have anything interesting to read and it's all by people who've been dead for donkey's years. It might have been interesting when they wrote it. When was *Le Grand Meaulnes* written?'

'Not long ago – it was published just before the war. And the author was very young, about twenty-five. He was killed in action. It was his only book.'

Peggy, already in love with the idea of the lost manor house, lost love, felt tears coming at the thought of the lost writer, given the chance to write only one wonderful book, dead with all his other books still unwritten. 'If I could read *Le Grand Meaulnes* I'd really work at it.'

'I'll see if I can get hold of it for you, and you could try asking your French mistress. Don't cry for him, Peg, he can still speak to us. Once something's written down, we've got it for ever. That's why burning books is a crime against the human soul. When does the school term start?'

'Tuesday after next.'

'So soon? I was going to suggest that you came and stayed with us for a few days. Wait till half term and then we'll have some fun. Cheer up, only a couple of months.'

'Could I really come and stay? Just me?'

'You don't want to haul Hilda along, do you? She's too elderly by half for me. No, come on your own and we'll be three girls about town.'

The thought of that was enough to keep Peggy happy on the drive home. They were back on the main road with the narrow twisting lanes behind them before Ted said, 'You

know, we don't even know the name of that place.' Stella
and Peggy exchanged glances; *their* secret.

She felt less happy when they got back and Stella went
into the sitting room with Mother for a few words. The
others, except for Hilda, were at the end of the garden,
hanging over the fence and waving to trains. Hilda was
martyring in the parlour with the mending pile, darning a
stocking; it was Peggy's, the one she had holed on the
shopping basket.

'You look like one of the Bisto Kids,' Hilda said. 'There
are grass stains on your skirt. At least comb your hair.'

Perhaps she ought to have paid more attention to what
Dorothy had been saying about grass stains. Methylated
spirits, wasn't it? It might have been quite a good article.
Why *had* she gone and mentioned blood . . . ?

'We had a lovely day.' She leaned against the door jamb,
one ear cocked towards the sitting room, listening for
scandalized shrieks or anguished sobs. 'You wouldn't have
liked it one bit. We took off our shoes and stockings and
played cricket.'

Hilda squinted at her needle to rethread it. 'Someone
had to stay with Mother.'

'She could have come if she'd wanted. Don't you think
she might like to be on her own sometimes. I do.'

'You can't go through life just doing what you want,'
Hilda said, evading the argument. It evidently had not
occurred to her that Mother might occasionally enjoy
being alone. Perhaps Hilda didn't enjoy her own company
very much. Why shouldn't you go through life just doing
what you wanted, so long as it made you happy and didn't

hurt anyone else? What was that thing they had in the United States? A constitution . . . *We hold these truths to be self-evident, that all men are created equal, that they are endowed by their Creator with certain inalienable rights, that among these are life, liberty and the pursuit of happiness.* How did you pursue happiness? This always made her think of herself crashing through a wood, ducking under branches, tripping over roots, brambles tearing at her skirt and, somewhere ahead, the sounds of Happiness, always just out of reach. Had the Americans caught it yet? From what she could tell by the films at the Electric Palace in the High Street, they had a lot more fun trying.

The sitting-room door opened and she heard Stella saying, 'I'd better round up the Summersby clan or we'll never get home before midnight.'

She must have gone through the French windows for it was Mother who came out into the hall, looking pale but composed, and went upstairs without seeing Peggy in the parlour doorway. At least, Peggy hoped that she had not seen her. The hall turned where the staircase ended; it was easy to miss someone you were not expecting to see. Or was Mother pretending not to see her because she didn't know what to say? How old had Mother been when she found out where babies came from, before she had known that they couldn't possibly be delivered in the doctor's bag? It *must* have been before she found she was expecting Hilda. How awful if it hadn't been.

Ollie, heading for the glories of King Edward's Grammar School on a scholarship, needed a new outfit. Peggy, resigned to making do with her own until Christmas at least, took out her school skirt and held it up against herself.

'I must have grown three inches since July, and all in the leg.'

'How much hem have you got left?' Hilda had not grown at all; there was barely an inch between them now.

'Not much, it's been turned down twice already.'

'Well, you can't wear it like that – it's almost up to your knees. Unless you want to pass for an Upper Third – the way you carry on you probably could. Pull the thread out, tack some binding on and make a false hem.'

'It'll look awful.'

'It will if *you* hem it. I'll do it on the machine, but you'll have to see to the tacking and binding. And don't forget that sheet that needs turning.'

'As if I could.'

'And you'd better do something about your hat.'

The hat looked worse than she remembered. Hilda's, when it was on, remained where she put it on her sleek head. Peggy's thicker, springier hair made hers creep upwards and she would tug it down on one side or the other, or smack it back into place. Dorothy always had her hats re-blocked at the beginning of each term. Peggy held hers over the kettle spout until the steam turned it limp and then moulded it back into some kind of hat shape, using a pudding basin as a block. The purple ribbon with the school crest had never recovered from being washed last year.

The school insisted on a winter uniform from the beginning of the autumn term, whatever the weather, for the look of the thing, presumably. Not that her summer straw hat was any better; it had frayed round the edge, like Huckleberry Finn's. Each term began like this, but autumn was the worst, everything smelling of mothballs, nothing fitting, and light, comfortable clothes packed away until April or May. She could still squeeze into last year's hockey shoes but the gym shoes she had been wearing all through the holidays would have to be replaced; her gym tunic was too short, but no one minded that, the shorter the better.

Why couldn't she get a job in the holidays like Maurice Hendry, and contribute to household expenses? If Mother worked, why shouldn't she? But Maurice's father was a milkman, he had very likely been able to put in a word for Maurice. If she found work she'd be taking it from someone who really needed it, for if men who had fought for their country had to sell matches in the street there were unlikely to be jobs going begging for schoolgirls who might be hard up but were never hungry. What was going to happen in four years' time, when she left school? The grandmothers had promised to put Hilda through university if she could get an exhibition; would they do the same for her? And if she couldn't get an exhibition, what then, a commercial career? That sounded fine and it probably would be for a man. For her it would mean a typewriter and a telephone to answer.

She never did badly at school, but she rarely did superlatively well, either. If she ever did come top of her form it was always at the end of a week in the middle of term, rather than at the end of the summer when the prizes were doled out. There was not one single distinguishing thing about her – except for the thing that she could tell to no one, that she seemed to have a wireless telegraph receiver in her head. The phantom telegraphist was still sending messages intermingled with those bursts of indecipherable vibrations that might be voices.

If only there was someone she could talk to about it, someone other than Stella, far away in London, which would mean using a public phone box while a restive queue formed outside. But she knew only too well what happened when you talked about things that other people were not ready to hear.

That was another cloud that spoiled the thought of going back to school. On the whole she was quite looking forward to it, but Dorothy would be there. She and Dorothy had sat next to each other all the way up the school, since they first met in the Upper IIIrd, sharing a double desk then; always being ticked off for swinging their feet because their legs were so short. What would Dorothy do if Peggy greeted her as usual and sat down at the next desk? Would she get up ostentatiously and move, as Mrs Prior had so deliberately cut Mother in church, causing everyone to wonder, secretly and out loud, what had happened between them. With luck Dorothy would not be able to bring herself to say anything.

The third black cloud on the horizon was the thought that Hilda might be made a prefect – only a sub-prefect in the Lower VIth, but even that was a promotion that would give her the right to extend her tyranny from home to school. Though tyranny, Peggy thought, was not quite the right word. You might defy a tyrant, defy him heroically even, become a martyr. There was no defence at all against Hilda's nagging; you could not, heroically or otherwise, defy anything so monotonous and petty. If a tyrant cried, 'Off with his head!' you might die nobly, refusing to submit. But if the tyrant said petulantly, 'Oh, go and clean your shoes, they're not fit to be seen,' what could you do but obey? Beheading could happen only once, nagging went on for ever.

The hat was drying out an even odder shape than it had been to begin with. The brim was almost frilly. She took the sewing shears that she had been using on the sheet, and trimmed off the worst part, but the blades bit further into the felt than she had intended, and the result was lopsided; quite dashing, really.

She tried it on and looked in the mirror; if she took off the school ribbon and trimmed it with one of those huge pre-war pompoms – and they were easy enough to make with wool – it would be an elegant winter *chapeau*. But not for school. She tried to even it up on the other side but the wretched thing was so misshapen that it was impossible to get an even trim all round, and now there was hardly enough of a brim to turn up, even to call a brim.

Would it still qualify as a school hat? There was no rule about the actual style of the hat so long as it was dark blue felt or velours of a sober design – as if anyone would turn up with a head full of ostrich plumes and silk roses. She might try to get away with it at school, but she would never get it past Hilda.

The autumn term began on Tuesday. Hilda, taking no

chances with the sub-prefecture, left the house early with scathing observations about people who rushed in at the last moment. Ollie was long gone, spurred by the spirit of adventure and anxious to start his new school life as soon as possible: new suit, new tie, new cap, new shoes. He would, of course, come home looking like Richmal Crompton's William, but no one would do any more than murmur a mild reproof. Boys were supposed to get untidy, it was part of their manhood, as getting them clean again was part, if not all, of womanhood. Hilda had a new hat after all; Peggy had Hilda's. By the time she had finished trying to refurbish the old one it was past saving.

'You couldn't even give it to the poor,' Hilda had said.

'Why would the poor want it?' Peggy said. She did not throw it away though. Fashions changed so fast; next year a hat with no brim might be absolutely *it*.

The school was on the edge of town, as far as it possibly could be from the dangerously virile territory of the grammar school, and the library was on the way, so Peggy walked along with Mother, feeling newly companionable. Stella's talk had done some good but it had taken Mother several days before she could say anything. In the end, when she and Peggy were alone in the garden, planting bulbs, she had said quietly, 'You know, darling, you were rather foolish with Dorothy. When you realized she didn't know what you were talking about ... wouldn't it have been kinder to tell her to ask her mother?'

Even now she was not looking at Peggy but rather harder than necessary at a clump of marguerites.

Peggy addressed the quince tree. 'If I'd done that she still

79

wouldn't know. Mummy, I *am* sorry about Mrs Prior last Sunday. I think she's an—'

'Peggy! Never mind what you think. She must be allowed to do as she feels best.'

'What, cutting you in church, in front of everybody?'

'I doubt if anyone else noticed,' Mother said. Unexpectedly she laughed, and as Peggy turned towards her their eyes met. 'Poor soul, she didn't even know how to cut me properly. She scurried off with the rest of the family in tow. It wasn't done at all well. She's not really built for cutting.'

'You didn't laugh last week,' Peggy said. They stopped pretending to garden and knelt facing each other.

'I was upset. I had no idea what was wrong with the wretched woman until Stella explained what had happened. Why did you tell her and not me?'

She had not thought of her mother being hurt by this; she had been trying to protect both of them, chiefly herself. 'It was Stella who explained to me all about babies and . . . that sort of thing.' She wondered if Mother knew just how much of that sort of thing Stella had explained. Not, she thought, the bit about contraception, courtesy of Dr Stopes.

'I asked her to because I thought she'd do it better . . . all her nursing experience. I left it much too late with Hilda. I suppose Mrs Prior didn't know what to do. I sent her a note, Peggy, apologizing for any upset, but I said I thought that young girls should know about such things these days as they are so much more independent and going out to earn their own livings. Stella suggested that. Mrs Prior will think I am frightfully fast and full of dangerous modern ideas.'

'You are,' Peggy said. They had never sat together and talked like this before. 'You are absolutely and utterly dangerous. No one is safe with you at large. Why don't you get a motorcycle and ride around town on it?'

'With you on the carrier? I was just wondering what we were going to do on Sunday – you're not going to hide away again?'

'I wasn't hiding, I really did have a toothache. But I might have invented one if it hadn't started hurting in time. I'll come with you this week. We'll brazen it out. You backed me up, I'll back you up – I honestly never thought that Mrs Prior would do anything to you, I was just worried about what Dot would say to me. Did Mrs P answer your note?'

'Not a word. Well, the ball is with her now, as they say.'

'Who's going to cut who?'

'Shouldn't that be *whom*? I shan't cut anybody,' Mother said. 'Anyone would think we were affronted duchesses.'

In the event they need not have worried. None of the Priors had been at matins; but there was still Dorothy to face today.

Chapter 6

There was a traffic jam in the entrance hall where notices were pinned up so that people could find out what form they would be in. Peggy looked first at the list of new appointments and there, halfway down the list of sub-prefects, was Hilda Hutton. So Hilda would be going solemnly up to the platform after prayers to receive her new hat ribbon from the hands of the headmistress herself. Which meant that Peggy could have her old one to go with the inherited hat. Joan Sykes was going to be Head Girl – well, that was all right. Joan was studious and serious, not one to go on all the time about the Good Name of the School, endlessly exhorting shirkers and slackers.

She checked the form lists, Lower V Beta first. If she looked at Alpha and her name was not there it would be a disappointment. It would be disappointing to be in Beta anyway, but if she looked there first she could be seen to be expecting it and someone might crow. No . . . she was not in Beta, and nor was Dorothy. They were both on the Alpha list.

She could admit only then that she had been secretly praying that one of them might have been squeezed out. They had both done pretty well last year, but others had done better. Still, here they were, together again.

She could not see Dorothy in the crowd around the

notice board. Pausing only to exchange greetings with people she knew she hurried down the corridor, almost colliding at the corner with Joan Sykes, who was talking, of all the bad luck, to Hilda.

'You weren't going to *run*, were you?' Hilda said, when the new head girl failed to bellow at her. 'Apologize at once to Joan.'

Peggy had in fact skipped aside at the last moment. She had not been running, the collision had not taken place, but the floor was newly polished and she was off-balance.

'I'm sorry,' she said. 'I wasn't running.'

'You were about to be.' Hilda was already in training. Oh, she *was* going to make herself disliked. 'You're in the Lower Fifth now.' As if Peggy did not know which form she was in. Anyway, being in the Lower Vth was not so very special; you still weren't a senior and it brought no privileges. You couldn't even come in by the front door until you were in the Upper Vth.

The Alpha form room was half full and Dorothy had not yet arrived. Peggy dropped her books on to a desk in the middle. 'Anyone bagged this yet?'

'No, go ahead,' several voices said. The desks on either side were still vacant. Now it was up to Dorothy, when she arrived, to decide whether to sit, as she had always done, alongside Peggy, or remove herself to another part of the room. If she did that, everyone would notice. Would Dorothy really want to risk that, and let herself in for having to explain if anyone said anything? Someone was bound to.

Olive Stapleton came in and sat on Peggy's desk. 'Had a good holiday?'

'Not bad. We didn't go anywhere, did you?'

'Only to Devon, my grandparents'. We got some decent riding. There's this darling little chestnut...'

Olive burbled on about withers and fetlocks and hogged manes. Peggy had only to listen and look tremendously interested while keeping one eye on the door. Other conversations drifted round her. People had been boating, cycling, one or two had gone abroad. All the time the room was filling up; all but three of the desks were occupied now. The one on her right had been claimed by Marjorie Shaw, who was new to the form, having got her Remove from Beta. Marjorie knew no better but everyone else was, by tacit consent, leaving the other desk for Dorothy. When was she going to appear? And there she was, in the doorway, looking across to the far side of the room.

It was too ridiculous. Peggy deliberately caught her eye before she could look away, and nodded towards the empty desk. *Don't be a bigger idiot than you can help, Dot. You'll have to explain. You don't want to do that, do you?*

Dorothy was evidently committed to being an idiot. She stared past Peggy and headed for the vacant desk by the window, at the same time as Daphne Roper wandered down the aisle to the one beside Peggy.

'I say, isn't Dot going to bag this one?'

'Doesn't look like it,' Peggy said.

Daphne made round eyes. 'But you two always . . .'

'She's off to fresh woods and pastures new,' Peggy said lightly.

'You can canter for absolutely *miles*,' Olive was saying.

'It must be glorious,' Peggy said fervently, as if Olive's

holiday exploits were the only thing worth talking about. 'I wish I could ride. It's not the same on a bike.'

'Have you got one, then?'

'No, just dreaming of it.' It was not difficult to make bicycles and horses sound the most interesting things in the world in this atmosphere. Either Daphne could see that she was enthralled or had the sense to realize that she was pretending to be. But that same atmosphere would be the cause when Daphne, as she certainly would, mentioned to some friend that Peggy Hutton and Dorothy Prior had fallen out and people, as if they had nothing better to do, would start to speculate and rumours would fly.

Miss Flower came in and all talk stopped instantly. She greeted them and ordered them to line up at the door to walk down the corridor to the hall, for prayers. The corridors were not wide. They walked in silent single file, following the form in front. What was going to happen the first time they made a crocodile and had to go in pairs? Pairs, like pigeons, seemed mated for life. If you suddenly changed your partner it was assumed that something terrible had come between you, and in any case, it was inconvenient, especially with even numbers in the form. If there was one over that person had to walk alongside the form mistress, but Alpha had even numbers this term. Unless Dorothy managed to prise apart another couple and insert herself she would be stuck with Peggy again.

Double idiot.

The first lesson was scripture. Daphne, posted at the door to close it behind incoming mistresses, mouthed, 'Ware corsets!' and they all rose silently as Miss Kelsey entered clutching her Bible and encased in the dress that she had bought new, according to popular slander, for Queen Victoria's funeral.

Miss Kelsey creaked as she moved. It was probably her elastic-sided boots but people professed to hear the twang of ancient whalebone. Whichever was true, she could be detected approaching from some distance. Rumour followed her. She was presumed to have some sinister hold over the headmistress, who would otherwise have pensioned her off before she became quite so obviously barmy. She had once taught Latin and now, put out to pasture in scripture, where she could do little damage, still addressed her classes in the way that had become a habit.

'*Salvete, puellae.*'

They chorused back, '*Salve tu quoque, Magistra.*'

'*Sedete.*'

They sat.

The scripture lessons rambled vaguely in Miss Kelsey's wake as she wandered from Old Testament to New, following a lesson on Ezekiel's visions with a tour through the Epistles of Paul the Apostle, adroitly skidding over verses that contained Certain Words. The deadly tedium could be relieved by reading ahead to see if any such as bowels or circumcision was coming up and wondering what evasive action Miss Kelsey would take. Girls who did not know what the words meant had learned that they were unspeakable because Miss Kelsey did not speak them. She could scarcely bring herself to pronounce the word 'womb' in 'O Come, All Ye Faithful'.

Miss Williams, at prayers, had made her customary speech to welcome them all back and instil fear into the new Upper IIIrds by listing her favourite prohibitions, starting with unpunctuality and the use of slang, and her particular abomination, the Electric Palace. 'I trust that no girl will be seen entering a cinematograph theatre wearing anything that identifies her with this school.'

Miss Kelsey pursued the theme with moist enthusiasm: films, especially American films, were Godless iniquities. This reminded her of Godless Bolsheviks and spiritualists, engaged in the Godless iniquity of trying to speak with the dead which led, five minutes before the bell rang, to her intended subject, the Witch of Endor in the Book of Samuel, raising the dead prophet for King Saul.

There was no point in ragging Miss Kelsey. After ten minutes no one had the energy to do anything but sit slack-jawed, heavy-eyed, waiting for it to be over; and a bad mark for scripture was treated with as much severity as a bad mark in algebra.

It was a relief to move on to French. As Miss Kelsey's creaking retreat faded into the distance Mlle Chardin's heel-taps approached smartly from the other direction.

'*Bonjour, mesdemoiselles.*'

'*Bonjour, Mam'zelle Chardin.*'

'*Asseyez-vous, s'il vous plaît.*'

Mlle Chardin was always faultlessly courteous. If words for please and thank you had ever existed in Latin they had not survived the decline and fall of the Roman Empire.

At the end of the lesson Peggy went up to Mlle

Chardin, partly so as to have an excuse to leave the room alone without having to wonder what Dorothy would do, and partly because she had a genuine question.

'Mam'zelle, my aunt told me about a book she'd read called *Le Grand Meaulnes*. Do you know it?'

'By Alain-Fournier. I do, Peggy. I am very fond of it. Have *you* read it?'

'No, but I'd like to.'

'In French?' Mlle Chardin's slender eyebrows rose. 'I do not know if it has been translated.'

'In French,' Peggy said, bravely.

'I'll see if I can find my copy. But Peggy, I must warn you, although it is about a schoolboy it was not written for children. You will have to work very hard if you want to enjoy it.'

Ah, but for once there would be a reason for working hard. So much of what they learned in school seemed to be of no practical use at all.

'*Merci, Mam'zelle.*' Peggy hurried, but did not quite run, to catch up with the others.

Dorothy avoided her all day with a scuttling furtiveness that at first wounded Peggy, who knew that everyone was watching and wondering, then infuriated her because it was ludicrous to watch and yet she could not laugh. But by the end of the afternoon the fury was turning to pity, which angered her even more because she did not see why she should have to feel sorry for Dorothy.

She and Hilda had never walked home together since the end of Peggy's first week at the High School. Hilda had then decided that there was no longer any need to keep an

eye on her little sister. That had been three years ago, Hilda
in the Upper IVth then, already too grand to be seen with
Upper IIIrds, but with no responsibilities for them either.

Now Hilda was involved with serious prefectly matters
in the VIth Form common room after school, and in any
case she would have been displeased if Peggy had suddenly
appeared at her side. Peggy and Dorothy had usually left
the premises with a group but, living in the same direction,
had always turned off and crossed the High Street
together. Their private split, which ought to have con-
cerned no one else at all, was already causing ripples in
Lower V Alpha. Even something as simple as walking
home would now have to be conducted like a military
campaign. Dorothy would not join a group that Peggy was
in, but as they all came down the drive Peggy risked giving
her one last chance to be sensible by attaching herself to
the usual crowd that included Dorothy, Daphne and Olive.
Before they were out of the gate it had broken up in an
awkward silence, Daphne and Olive uncertain which of
them to stick with and wandering off alone. Dorothy
grabbed Edith Rowland's arm and quickened her pace,
talking animatedly.

Peggy looked at her watch and crossed the road, as if she
had an urgent appointment in another direction.

'How was school?' Mother asked brightly, when she
came in.

There was no need to ask Hilda, who was stitching on
her new hatband with demonstrative piety, as though by
becoming a sub-prefect she had taken a vow of chastity,
like a nun.

'I'm still in Alpha,' Peggy said, eyeing the discarded ribbon. 'I say, Hilda, is that going begging?'

Hilda tossed it across. 'You'll have to sew it on yourself.'

Peggy would have liked to tell Mother about what had happened in form, but they all had an unspoken agreement not to bother her with things unless they were really important. And Hilda, who was not aware of the facts, would be sure to say something unsympathetic.

In the kitchen Ollie was foraging for biscuits, his satchel slung on his arm.

'Had a good day?' Peggy said.

Ollie turned, furtive as a burglar. 'Oh yes. Ripping.'

'Do you think you'll like it at King Edward's?'

'Yes.' He thriftily returned one of the biscuits to the tin.

'I'm not counting. Is David in your form?'

'Who?'

'Mrs Hendry's David.'

'Oh, *Hendry*. Yes.' He was strangely unforthcoming. 'I've got loads of prep,' he added, boastfully slapping the satchel by way of an excuse to leave, and dodged past her to go upstairs. Peggy noticed that he was clutching a handful of cigarette cards. Ollie was always at a disadvantage when it came to swapping and trading these, coming as he did from a family of women who did not smoke. Stella sometimes remembered to pass him hers and Irene's, but his collection was pitiably thin, without a full set of anything yet. He must have found a generous friend, David perhaps, but he was unlikely to divulge any details. He and David were Hutton, O., and Hendry, D., now, entering a world of men, and Ollie would guard its secrets as jealously as any Freemason.

And yet, she thought later, weren't they all doing that? Ollie was no more secretive than she was. Those big families she read about in books and saw in films, where everyone grew up together and grew old together, sharing their joys and sorrows, and their secrets, they had gone for good, if they had ever existed. If someone had asked her, 'Do you love your family?' she would have replied, 'Of course,' but weren't they really becoming less a family than four friendly strangers whose joys and sorrows and secrets were fiercely concealed?

And not always so friendly.

She watched them as the days passed, as September darkened into October, and in bed, trying to keep the Morse at bay, she wondered about them.

What did she know of Mother, not as a mother but as a woman? Why should Ollie tell Peggy anything? She never confided in him; if she did he would not be interested. If she went up to the attic now and told him about her secret radio receiver he might be fascinated, but on the other hand he might equally think that she was mad and wonder why she had picked on him for such a shameful revelation. Mother would immediately think of tinnitus or worse and start worrying. Why not? Wasn't that what mothers were for? But she did not want to be worried about. It would be an imposition, making her feel guilty. Hilda would accuse her of trying to draw attention to herself. She couldn't even have a toothache without Hilda thinking that she was showing off. Stella was her only hope, Stella who never criticized, never worried, never nagged; always to be trusted. She could tell Stella everything, and when she wrote to her, she did.

Once she could have talked to Dorothy – or could she? Had she ever told Dorothy anything truly private? But Dorothy too was gone for good.

It would have been more bearable if she had left the school. Peggy would have felt lonely, bereft, but no one would have been surprised. If they had had a blazing row, in front of everybody, the other girls would have understood. But Dorothy's stealthy disengagement had left everybody confused. People were beginning to talk, not chattily but in a puzzled way, because it was somehow understood that it was Dorothy who had broken off the friendship but refused to say why. What could Peggy have *done*? No one asked her.

The crocodile problem had solved itself. Peggy did not witness the negotiations that had ended in Dorothy walking with Edith, but she had found herself paired naturally with Marjorie, the newcomer who sat at the next desk. Since Marjorie's friends had all been left behind in Lower V Beta she kept to herself and worked hard. Peggy, also forced to keep to herself, found that she was doing the same. It gave her something else to think about and after a while, without actively trying to, she began to pick up Commendations for her work.

For a time she heard nothing but amiable insults like 'Swot', but one Wednesday, after hockey, when they were in the cloakroom changing their shoes, Peggy overheard on the other side of a wall of hanging coats a voice, Daphne's, saying, 'But why?'

And Dorothy: 'My mother doesn't really approve. She said it might be healthier to have a wider circle of friends.'

Peggy was tempted to put her head between the coats; not to say anything – her sudden appearance would be enough to startle them into confusion.

'Healthier?' Daphne said. 'Whatever could she mean?'

'Peggy's not awfully lady-like sometimes,' Dorothy muttered.

Lady-like? Which of them *was* lady-like? The word came out of the Ark. It was all very well for a fossil like Mrs Prior to use it but didn't Dorothy understand what an ass she sounded, repeating it? Peggy knew exactly what was understood by it, and now that Daphne had got hold of the idea it might spread around Lower V Alpha and out through the school.

The conversation dwindled as Daphne and Dorothy left the cloakroom. They had to go back to the form room to collect prep. Peggy was left alone among the coats in that unique hush that fell always just before the last bell rang at the end of the afternoon and – *ditditdit-dit-ditdit-ditditdit*.

She said, furiously, 'Who's there?' but of course, no one answered.

She was the first one home. Mrs Hendry had been and gone and the house smelled of polish. She took off her hat and hung it up instead of tossing it towards the hall stand. She could always remember to take care of things while they were new. Even though Hilda had had this one first it was still presentable, and the ribbon did not look as if it had been chewed by a slavering maniac.

There were letters on the table, bills mostly – it was strange how you could tell from the outside – one from Granny Holt, she knew the writing, and one for her with a London postmark. She knew the writing on that, too: Stella's.

A letter? Stella sent postcards usually, dashed off in her big looping hand which never gave her room to say anything important. What could she have to tell Peggy that was important enough to need more room than a postcard? There was one from her to Mother, too. She could have put them both in one envelope and saved on the extra stamp. So Peggy's must be extra private.

She took the letter into the kitchen. She was thirsty and it would take too long to make tea. The milk did not smell fresh enough to drink on its own. She drew a glass of water from the cold tap that set the pipes yammering, and went down the garden. It was still mild enough to sit under the quince tree on the bench and read Stella's letter.

A train snuffled by in the cutting. She ought to have opened the envelope with a paper knife, neatly, as Mother and Hilda would. Instead she bit off the corner and ripped it open the way Ollie did on the rare occasions that anyone sent him a letter. It was not long.

Hullo, Old Thing [it began]. Remember I asked you if you'd like to come up to Town for the half? Well, how about next weekend instead (the 20th)? We might go to the theatre and meet some interesting people. Do find the time; you could come straight after school on Friday.

Love to all, Stella. PS If you have stacks of prep bring it along. We'll do it together.

Stella's writing was so extravagant that it filled up both sides of the little sheet and the postscript crawled up the side and round the top. Peggy sat looking at it. A visit to London would be wonderful if Mother would let her go; this must be what she was writing to Mother about. Stella seemed really anxious that Peggy should know personally how much Stella wanted her to come, as if Peggy might find reasons not to, otherwise. How could she think that?

There was no mention of Hilda. Hilda would not want to visit Stella but she was sure to find some objection to Peggy's going, and she might secretly resent it, like poor Jo March in *Good Wives*, dying to go to Europe and then seeing her youngest sister invited instead.

Indoors again she took another look at the other letter to make sure that the writing really was Stella's. Mother would be home early this week – it wouldn't be long before it was all discussed and settled.

As she went upstairs the front door rattled and Ollie came in. Even from above she could tell that something was wrong. Instead of exploding through the door and slamming it behind him he closed it quietly, hung up his cap and went along the hall to the kitchen without looking up to see her standing at the turn of the stairs. At the beginning of term he had embarked on his first day at the grammar school so full of hope and excitement and confidence. He had returned that evening less effervescent and, now she came to think of it, his homecoming each day had been quieter than the one before. He was creeping along the hall now like one of a beaten army, the sole survivor of a rout.

She called out quietly, 'Ollie?'

He reappeared in the hall below her.

'How was school today?'

'Ripping,' he said without enthusiasm.

He looked up briefly and she saw that he had a bruise on his cheekbone, just below the left eye. His new jacket looked dustier than it should have been.

'Been in a fight?'

'No,' he snapped, and went back into the kitchen. Had he been in a fight? No, he would have admitted to that; even if he'd lost, an honourable defeat would have been nothing to be ashamed of and a routine rough-house with the Central School boys was only to be expected. Perhaps he had been bullied, not by seniors like Flashman in *Tom Brown's Schooldays*, but by boys only a little older than himself, getting their own back for the bullying they had received when they were new bugs. Poor Ollie, coming home to a house full of women, Mother and sisters instead of Dad and brothers, only aunts and grannies instead of uncles who could jolly him into telling what had happened and give kindly advice.

Whatever she said to him would be dismissed as slop because she was a girl. Ollie could scarcely remember a time when there had been a man in the house; he had grown up among women who earned their own livings, managed their own money, kept things going, and yet he had to tell himself that they must be sloppy because they *were* women.

But then a man or an elder brother might be utterly unsympathetic and full of bracing nonsense about taking it on the chin; don't be a milksop, don't be a sneak. That was the rule – never be a sneak. And who made that rule? The bullies.

He might unburden himself to Mother, who he still called Mummy in unguarded moments, if she knew in advance what could have happened. She ought to know, even if he didn't tell her. Peggy thought she might mention it when they discussed Stella's letter.

Chapter 7

Mother and Hilda were talking in the hall.

'I got some beautiful herrings at lunch time,' Mother was saying, 'but of course I had to keep them in my basket. I think the whole library smelled of fish. Still, they were very fresh, we'll have them grilled for supper.'

Hilda was going through the letters. 'Six for you.'

'Bills. I don't want to look.'

'No, one's from Granny Holt and – this looks familiar.'

'Stella. Well, neither of them will be asking for money. Let's make tea and I'll read them in comfort.'

Peggy finished her algebra, ruled a neat line – you could lose marks if you forgot the line and more if it was a wavering one – closed her books and went down in time to hear Hilda saying, 'London? Next week? Oh, I don't think—'

She opened the kitchen door sharply. 'Sorry I didn't come down sooner, I was finishing my prep.'

'I suppose that means you scamped it,' Hilda said.

'No I didn't. I just got on with it as soon as I came in.' That's one in the eye for you, Hilda. You never do yours till after supper. 'I made a resolution. I'm always going to do that in future, except on Fridays.'

'That won't last long.'

'I've had a letter from Stella,' Mother said. 'She's asking

98

if you can go up to Town and visit her next weekend. Are you two plotting something?'

'Plotting? Of course not. But when she was here with Irene she asked if I'd like to go and I would, ever so.'

'Yes, but wasn't that going to be in the half?'

'You can't just go off to London in the middle of term,' Hilda said.

'At a weekend. Why not? I shouldn't miss any lessons. And I'd do my prep while I was there. We wouldn't be going out all the time.'

'Going out? Is all this arranged?'

'Stella wrote to me, too,' Peggy said. 'Just a note, asking if I'd like to come.'

'But why *next* weekend?' Hilda said. 'It's all very sudden.'

Why were they so suspicious, and what had it to do with Hilda anyway? But she must not lose her temper and upset Mother.

'You know how busy Stella is – and Irene. I expect it turned out they couldn't manage any time over the half but they can next weekend. I'll be much busier then, too. You know how everything piles up as term goes on.'

'Well, I haven't got time,' Hilda said.

'Has she written to you as well?' Peggy wrestled not to let her dismay show. Stella hadn't said anything about Hilda.

'You can't go on your own.'

'Why ever not?'

'To London? On a train?'

'I don't think that's going to be a problem,' Mother said mildly. 'Girls of Peggy's age travel halfway across the country to get to boarding schools.'

'They're used to it.'

'Yes,' Peggy said, 'because they start much younger. And Stella would meet me at Charing Cross. Even if she didn't I'd only have to take the Underground – it's straight through from Trafalgar Square to Baker Street. I've been to London before, we both have. We didn't get lost or robbed or murdered. People do actually live there, Hilda; people like us. They go shopping, they go to school, they aren't lying in lifeless heaps on street corners, are they?'

'We can talk about it later,' Mother said. 'I've got herrings for supper. What shall we have with them?'

'Bread and butter's nicest with herrings,' Peggy said, 'and there's not so much washing up.'

'You would say that,' Hilda hissed as Mother went out. 'And you're not to bother her with this London nonsense. I know the way you wheedle when you want something. Like just now, coming over all pious because you'd finished your prep. It doesn't fool *me*.'

'You only say it's nonsense because you haven't been asked. I bet if Stella had invited you, you'd be off like a shot. Green-eyed monster.'

'I certainly would not,' Hilda said. 'I don't think it's suitable.'

'Suitable? What do you mean?'

'You wouldn't understand.'

'Try me.'

'You're too young.'

'Too young to go to London or too young to know what you're getting at? You're always so *down* on Stella.'

'When you're older you'll know what I mean.'

They were muttering at each other so that Mother should not overhear. She hated it when they quarrelled but Hilda never had the sense to see that if she did not needle Peggy so often there would be fewer quarrels.

'You're not at school now,' Peggy said. 'If Mother wanted a sub-prefect here she'd have made you one long ago.'

'Any more cheek from you – where are you going?' as Peggy turned to the door. 'You are *not* to bother Mother when she's so tired.'

'Oh, *shut up*, jaw-me-dead,' Peggy spat, and ran up the stairs so that if Hilda wanted to retort she would have to shout.

Mother's door was ajar. Peggy tapped and looked round it.

'Can I have a word?'

'I said we could talk about it later.'

'Not that, not London,' Peggy said. 'Have you seen Ollie?'

'Isn't he home yet? I thought he must have gone out again, he usually does.'

'He's in his room.'

'Are you sure? I can't hear anything.'

'He came in just after I did. I think he – I don't think he's had a very nice day. Or a very nice week. And if you ask him he'll just clam up.'

'What happened?'

'Oh, he didn't tell *me* anything, that's the trouble; he won't tell anyone. Not us, anyway. He needs a big brother, someone who'd *know*, without having to ask. I think

101

someone's been hitting him, you know what little beasts boys can be.'

'Not girls?'

'Beastlier, but not in the same way.'

'Dorothy—?'

'Just idiotic, don't worry about that. I was going to say, we'd better not pump poor Ollie. It'll only make him miserable – more miserable.'

'But if I don't say anything he'll think I don't care.'

'And if you do he'll growl. But when he growls don't say anything else – and, Mummy . . .'

'Yes, darling?'

'Don't let Hilda go on at him for being rude. It's not rudeness and it'll only make him worse.' She laughed. 'Look what it does to me.'

'I know. You can be very wise sometimes, Peggy.'

'I don't feel wise.'

'Of course not. If you felt wise at your age you'd be a dreadful prig. Do you think you can manage to get to London without being murdered or kidnapped by White Slavers?'

'You'll let me go?'

'So long as you don't scrimp your prep I don't see why not.'

'I'll work twice as hard. Mummy, thank you. I'll love you for ever.' Peggy threw her arms round her.

'You great bear, you're taller than I am. Go down and help Hilda with those herrings – put her in a good mood.'

At the door Peggy paused. 'Mother, what *is* White Slave Traffic?'

'Oh, now what have I said?' Mother was blushing, but she looked amused. 'Ask Stella. She'll tell you and never turn a hair.'

She felt that she could not wait to see Stella, now that she knew she was going to. All the while curiosity in Lower V Alpha was building like pressure in a gasbag – she had to face it daily. Since it was Dorothy who had detached herself then obviously it was Peggy's fault.

Which it was, if you could call it a fault. Why would no one ask?

During Friday lunch hour, after Dorothy had got up and left a table in the library when Peggy sat down at it, Marjorie came right out and said, 'What *has* happened between you two?'

'It's private,' Peggy said. She was beginning to like Marjorie, who was friendly and straightforward. No one else would have put the question point blank. But they had never confided in one another. She didn't know how to answer, after waiting so long for the question.

'Well, it isn't private, you know. It's blighting the atmosphere. You don't want a schism, do you?'

'A what?'

'At the rate we're going the whole form will split, half on your side, half on Dorothy's.'

'They'll be loony if they do. I never heard anything so stupid. Why should people have to take sides when it's nothing to do with them?'

'I know it's loony, but that won't stop it happening.'

'What does Dorothy say?'

'I haven't asked her.'

'Why don't you?'

'It wouldn't be loyal – to you.'

Peggy's warm response to the thought that Marjorie was being loyal to her faded rapidly. 'So you're on my side.'

'Well, of course.'

'I see what you mean about taking sides,' Peggy said. 'It just happens. Well, don't feel disloyal, Marj – ask her.'

'I needn't, actually,' Marjorie said. 'Daphne did ask her, and she told me.'

'What did she tell you?'

'She says her mother thinks you aren't a nice person to know.'

This must have been the conversation she had overheard in the cloakroom after hockey. 'Unlady-like?'

'Er . . . yes. What have you done?'

'I haven't *done* anything,' Peggy sighed. 'It was something I said. I told Dorothy about something she didn't know, something she ought to know.'

'Babies?'

'What makes you say that?'

'It's the only unlady-like thing I could think of, apart from eating in the street.'

'It was partly that.' Marjorie looked reassuringly unshocked. 'Do *you* know?'

'Yes . . . not everything,' Marjorie said, cautiously.

'You know about monthlies, then.'

'Yes, I've started. Have you?'

'Yes.'

'Is that what you told Dot?'

'Marj, I had to. She could start any day and she didn't know a thing. She'd have been terrified. And her mother's such a jellyfish; you'd think she'd be grateful but she cut *my* mother in church and now all the Priors have started going to evensong instead of matins, just to avoid us. I didn't mean to tell her anything, I just – I can't even remember what I said, but I could see she didn't understand. And I couldn't let her think that women have periods for nothing, that's why I told her about babies.'

'Our maid calls it the Curse of Eve,' Marjorie said. 'It's a sort of punishment for being a woman. You know, in Genesis, God telling Eve, "I will greatly multiply thy sorrow, in sorrow thou shalt bring forth children," because she tempted Adam.'

'That's what Adam said – "It wasn't my fault, God. The woman tempted me." We've only got his word for it.'

'Sssh.' Marjorie giggled. 'Don't start making fun of the Bible or they'll think you're an atheist, too. Kelsey would have forty fits. Do you think Kaiser Bill would expel you?'

'For being an atheist? I don't know. Probably being unlady-like is much worse.'

'You know, it is loony, absolutely loony. We're all girls here, it's going to happen to all of us.'

'Well, if anyone asks you what I did you can tell them. I'm not ashamed. And they *will* ask you – Olive and Daphne are watching us now. Look, over there. Just like stuffed owls.'

'No . . . I don't think I'd better do that,' Marjorie said. 'You never know how people will take it. But I think you were a brick. And Dorothy's a blithering idiot. She ought to be jolly glad you told her.'

'That's what I thought,' Peggy said, gloomily.

'Well, cheer up. Aren't you going somewhere nice? I saw you had a bag in the cloakroom.'

'London – straight after school. I'm staying with my aunt.'

'Oh, *jammy*. A whole weekend?'

'If I don't fall into the hands of White Slavers.'

They both laughed.

'Do you know what a White Slaver is?'

'No, do you? I bet it's something else unlady-like.'

'It must be,' Peggy said, 'or we'd know. I'll tell you when I get back.'

Hilda came out from behind a bookcase and gave them both an order mark for making too much noise in the library.

The London train was already in the station when Peggy reached it. She had left school in plenty of time but on the way through town she fell in behind a scuffling group of grammar school boys, small ones, Ollie among them. They were not behaving like the little gentlemen they were supposed to be, but they were not actually fighting and they all seemed to be enjoying themselves.

Peggy knew better than to address Ollie by name, revealing the embarrassing fact that he had a sister, and crossed the street before, she hoped, he had time to notice her, but as she passed Boots, on the corner of Station Road, she heard a familiar voice, not directed at her, but carrying.

'See you on Monday! I'm going to the station – to watch trains.'

There were friendly, slightly envious jeers. The other boys were expected home for tea where mothers would be awaiting them.

She did not stop for him – anyone might be watching – but slowed down a little so that he could catch up with her if he wanted to. He did, but not until they were almost at the station and everyone else was out of sight.

'You didn't say anything to Mum, did you?'

'What about?'

'*You* know. The other day. When I'd got that bruise.'

'Bit of bullying, was it?'

'A bit. It's all right now. My friend Hendry, his big bro's in the Sixth. He sorted them out.'

That must be Maurice Hendry. Three cheers for *him*. The next best thing to a big brother was a pal with a big brother. Clearly Maurice had not wasted any time before coming to the rescue.

'Who did he sort out?'

'Oh, some types in the Lower Fourth.'

'I didn't know you and Dav— Hendry were friends.'

'Oh yes, for ages.' That must be all of a month. 'He's going to join our Scout Troop. I say, thanks for keeping quiet – to Mum, I mean. She'd only have fussed.'

Peggy had to let that pass. 'You're welcome. Did you really want to watch the trains? I'll stand you a platform ticket and you can go up on the bridge. Don't you see enough trains at home?'

'It's not the same,' Ollie said; 'not when they're at the end of the garden. And all they do is go past. I like the station – all the noise and barrows and milk churns, and you can go up close to look at the engines and watch them shunting. I'd like to be a station master.'

'Not an engine driver? That's what most boys are supposed to want.'

'Yes, but then you've only got one train. I say, Mum's letting you go to London, do you think she'd let me?'

'What, now?'

'No, some other time, with a friend.'

'She might, but wait until I come back in one piece. Ask nicely, and if she says no, don't nag. Give her time to think about it. Where would you want to go?'

'Clapham Junction,' Ollie said. 'Dozens of trains, thousands of trains. You can see them coming from all directions.'

'Yes, and there's mine. Here's the penny.'

'Thanks, sis; you're all right.' Ollie sped towards the platform ticket machine. Peggy went to the window to buy her return and sprang aboard as the train began to move. She looked out and up as they went through the cutting to recognize her own garden fence by the quince tree hanging over it. Alongside, the telegraph wires, strung between their poles, carried their invisible, inaudible messages. The train was making far too much noise for her to hear anything now, Morse code or voice, wheezing, gasping, the carriages rocking, the wheels clacking over points and joints in the rails. As it gathered speed the sounds began to blur together into a regular rhythmic purr. It was like being inside a large, happy cat.

As soon as she sat down she began to feel more grown up and worldly, even in her school coat and hat. The compartment was empty and the carriage had no corridor, so she could be sure that no one else would be joining her before the next station. In her bag was a spare hair ribbon, one of those wide ones that Ollie called a flapper, wide enough to hide the school hatband and its crest. She wrapped the ribbon round it and tucked the ends in. Now it was just a hat, not wildly stylish but, having been Hilda's until recently, it was still hat-shaped.

She untied the end of her plait and combed it out until she could see in the mirror above the seat that it rippled down her back and curled up at the ends. The bow that fastened it matched the one round the blue felt hat. She took off the school tie and pinned in its place a brooch she had brought along specially. It was large and round and flat with a boss in the middle like a Viking's shield, one of those things that lay around the house, always turning up in drawers, belonging to nobody.

It might have been owned by an aunt or left by a visitor. No one ever wore it and, pinning it on, she could see why, but it hid the naked top button of her blouse that was normally under the knot of her tie. Oh, to be in the VIth where you could wear a proper blouse with a V-neck and no tie. And oh, for a new skirt. She had stitched braid round the worn line of the hem where her school skirt had been let down. The braid hid the pale thready track but everyone knew why it was there. If she had had time she would have changed before she left school, but the next train left an hour later, which would have meant a whole hour less in London. She would change when she reached the flat, where Stella would give her advice on how to look chic.

The train jolted to a halt. They were not in a station so the signal must be against them – there was another line curving in on the right. It was very quiet. Beyond the window, on a distant road, carts and cars were passing but she could not hear them, not even that heavy motor lorry. A biplane crossed the sky, quite low – there must be an aerodrome near by – but it passed as silently as a glider. After the racket of the moving train it was almost like being deaf, and then the Morse started up, *dit–dit–ditdit-dit-dit*. Could it be a message, a message for her? Who could be sending it? Or was it leaking mysteriously from the telegraph wires? They were quite low here, on short poles, out in the open. *Dit–dit–ditditdit–ditdit–dit* . . .

There was laughter in the next compartment, the engine gushed steam and with a lurch the train trundled on, over the points, into the next station.

Three young men got in. For the first time Peggy remembered Hilda's warning, one of Hilda's many warnings: 'Make sure you travel in a ladies' compartment.' She had not even thought to look for one; there probably weren't such things on trains like this. What would Hilda do? Get out quickly, no matter how rude that looked, and find a compartment with a woman in it? The men seemed respectable enough, probably clerks, but they were sitting by the other window, muttering to each other and looking sideways at her. It was too late to get out now – the train was moving again.

The one who was sitting on her side of the compartment leaned over, raised his hat and said, 'Excuse me, miss. Do you mind if we smoke?'

110

As the word SMOKING was etched on the window glass Peggy felt flattered that they should think it only polite to ask her permission.

'Of course not. Please do.'

'Thanks. D'you want one?' He held out the packet. His friend jogged his elbow, mouthing, 'Shut it, Jacko. She's only a kid.'

They all grinned at each other. Peggy felt her face turn pink and stared out of the window. Even without the tie and the hatband they could see how young she was.

'Sorry, miss,' Jacko said. 'No offence meant.'

'What, for offering me a cigarette or calling me a kid?' Peggy said. Was that a mistake? Ought she to ignore them? Hilda would.

'Both,' Jacko said. 'No hard feelings?'

'No hard feelings.'

The atmosphere grew very formal and they did not speak to her again. One of them got out a newspaper and they all bent over it, discussing something; it seemed to be greyhounds. Peggy did not know whether to feel relieved or disappointed. They were certainly not gentlemen but they were kind and well-mannered – not that Hilda would have thought so. Hilda would have said they were being familiar when they were only being friendly. She wished she knew how to behave; they might have had fun talking to each other and now they thought she was stuck-up and prissy. Hilda, no doubt, would have suspected them of being White Slavers in disguise.

The train ground slowly over the Hungerford Bridge into

Charing Cross Station. Looking up-river through the girders Peggy saw London and the Thames, murky in the evening light; even the new County Hall where Stella worked. Wordsworth had written, *Earth hath not anything to show more fair*. He'd been standing on Westminster Bridge, the next one along, but he must have seen what she was seeing, from the other direction. *All bright and glittering in the smokeless air*. Was London ever smokeless these days? The sky was yellow. Wordsworth had been there first thing in the morning.

They crept under the dirty glass arch and stopped and immediately there were hundreds of people surging towards the train, office workers, anxious to go home, the weekend before them. Peggy struggled through the crowds, one of the few who were going the other way. The three clerks had got off already at London Bridge. If Stella had not managed to meet her she would have to take the Tube – Trafalgar Square Underground Station was a couple of minutes' walk away – but there was Stella, just behind the ticket collector, waving.

The last time Peggy had seen her was on the day of the surprise picnic, in her blue-and-white summer frock. Now she wore a long coat with a huge velvet collar like a shawl, and a stunning wide-brimmed hat with a deep velvet band that matched the collar.

'Oh, what a hat!' Peggy cried.

'Pleased to see me or the hat?' Stella said. 'And come to that, where did you get yours? Where *did* you get that tile?'

'Is it that bad? I came straight from school. I tried to disguise it.'

112

'So I see. When I saw you butting through the throng with that hand bag I thought, A governess, off to her first position, clutching her pitiful belongings—'

'Don't rub it in. I don't look like a governess, do I? Oh, Stella—'

'Take it off, do. The sky won't fall if you go bare-headed for half an hour. That's better. Give me the case – is that your school bag too?'

'I had to bring it with me. My prep—'

'We'll get that out of the way tomorrow morning. This evening we'll go to the theatre. How long does it usually take you?'

'The prep? A couple of hours.' They were battling their way out of the station against the tide of home-going workers.

'Two of us should be able to manage it in one. Is there anything else you'd like to do?'

'Oh, anything. Just being in London's a treat.'

'Museums? Galleries? Concerts? Kew?'

'Kew?'

'The Botanical Gardens. Wonderful hothouses.'

'Anywhere. Ought I to send Mother a postcard?'

'If you like, but I said I'd telegraph if you *didn't* arrive.'

'That would have cheered her up no end. Hilda's sure I'll come to grief.'

'Won't she be terribly disappointed? Here we are, Trafalgar Square.'

Chapter 8

The flat was exactly as she had imagined it, just what she was planning for herself; up two flights of stairs to its own front door with the nameplate beside it, HOLT AND SUMMERSBY, as if they were partners in a firm. The hall led into a sitting room with bright curtains, a little kitchen, a tiny bathroom, so tiny that it seemed to have been built around the bath. The bedroom was reached through the sitting room, where vases of bronze chrysanthemums stood on white-painted bookshelves. The table in the bay window was where she herself would have put it, with a bowl of fruit that looked as if it had been chosen for the colours: apples, plums, tangerines. Peggy stood in the middle and rotated, looking at everything, the prints on the walls, the red Turkey carpet, the patchwork of cushions on the couch, the brightness, and lightness. Everything at home seemed so heavy and dark.

Stella, in the kitchen, called out, 'Leave all your things in the bedroom. We'll have tea before we do anything else.'

There were two beds. Peggy took off her coat and joined Stella in the kitchen.

'Where shall I sleep?'

'The sainted Irene has given up her bed. She'll camp on the divan in the sitting room.'

'Divan?'

'That sofa with no ends to it.'

'Oh, I couldn't—'

'Yes you can. It's meant to double as a bed, that's why it's so flat. Anyway, remember we've slept in army huts. Irene offered, so don't feel guilty. She won't be in till late, she's gone to a party meeting.'

'A party or a meeting?'

'Labour Party, it's a political meeting. There's a general election coming up. So, where would you like to go this evening?'

'I'd just as soon stay here,' Peggy said, 'it's so cosy and private. And just talk.'

'Really? Well, I'd like that too. We can go to a matinée tomorrow, there's something I really must take you to see.'

'What about tomorrow night?'

'Oh, I've got something planned for tomorrow night. I'll tell you later.'

'Something nice?' Peggy was so confident that it would be nice that she was slightly taken aback when Stella said, 'Something interesting.'

'When they say that at school it usually means something dull and difficult. "This will be really interesting, girls," and it turns out we're going to read Sir Walter Scott or study the life of the crested newt.'

'You don't care for Scott? What about *Ivanhoe*?'

'It would be all right if it didn't take so frightfully long for anyone to do anything. They spend so much time jawing you stop caring what happens to them.'

'I'm not going to subject you to an evening of Walter Scott, if that's what you're afraid of. No, it's just some

115

people I'd like you to meet. Take the tray through, will you? I'll bring the teapot.'

'This is just how I thought it would be,' Peggy said. They sat at the table in the bay window, looking down at the darkening street. 'You've even got a pillar box on the corner.'

'What made you think we would have?'

'It was one of your letters, posted late. I could just imagine you running out last thing to put it in the pillar box.'

'You must be clairvoyant.'

'What's that?'

'Able to see things that aren't actually in front of you. Clear-sighted, I suppose it meant in French, originally.'

'No, but when I'm grown up, this is what I want, a flat of my own to share with a friend. And I always picture it in a street like this with a pillar box on the corner – and me going out at night to post a letter.'

'I have to admit I've gone across in my dressing gown before now,' Stella said. 'You're not clairvoyant, are you?'

'Seeing things that aren't there? No. Hilda says that half the time I don't see things that are right under my nose.'

'Never mind Hilda. But you hear things, don't you? Is that still happening? That last letter you sent . . .'

Peggy had a feeling that this was really what Stella had wanted to talk about.

'Yes, it is – not all the time. I mean, it might be happening all the time, but I only notice when it goes quiet. On the train coming up we stopped just outside a station and for a minute or two I could hear it then, because all the other sounds seemed to have stopped, but it wasn't very loud and I don't know whether it started then or if I was just starting to hear it.'

'Still the Morse code?'

'That's what's so infuriating. Knowing it means something and that I might understand it if I could only keep up. And I can't. It does sound like someone going at forty words a minute. I can't even write it down. I've learned the code now – I can tap about five words a minute – with the end of a pencil. But they have to be very short words.'

'You never hear anything else? Didn't you say something about voices?'

'That's the funny thing, I'm not sure. Sometimes it almost sounds like voices. Not when the code's going but in between.'

'What sort of voices? People talking? One person talking?'

'I thought it might be singing once, but usually it's talk. But that doesn't happen very much and it's only *like* singing, *like* talking. I can never make out words, it's just *like* words.'

'Never names?'

'My name? Hello Peggy? I can't tell what it is, the way the sounds come out. It's a sort of vibration.'

'Do you concentrate?'

'I have to, but I don't want to. I try to crowd it out: you know, if you don't want to hear what people are saying to you in real life, you can hum, but it doesn't work with this – unless I really do hum, out loud. But that's no good when I'm trying to go to sleep. If only I knew where it was coming from. It's in my head, so far in. But so clear. I think, Why can't anyone else hear it?'

'Perhaps they can,' Stella said. 'More tea? Do have another cake, Irene bought them specially.'

'I meant, hear what's in *my* head, coming out through my skull, not hearing it in their own,' Peggy said. 'If they can they never say anything. Perhaps they're like me, afraid people will think they're mad.'

'You don't think you're mad, do you?'

'No. *And* I don't think I'm a witch.'

'Who said anything about witches?'

'The only person I could think of who heard voices talking was Joan of Arc, and you know what happened to her. But her voices told her to do things. That's what happens when you hear those sorts of voices, isn't it? They tell you to do things that you wouldn't usually do – that no one would do. That's when other people start to notice.'

'Do you know what a medium is?'

'Medium? Something in the middle, not very bad, not very good?'

'A person – but yes, the same idea, some*one* in the middle.'

'What, halfway between being slightly mad and very mad?'

'No, no. Forget about madness. Think of them as a sort of go-between—'

'Between what?'

Stella, elbows on the table, cupped her chin in her hand and looked down into the street. 'Between this world and the next. The other side.'

The other side of what? What next world? The conversation was turning churchy, the last thing she would have expected from Stella. She herself had stopped expecting heaven to be angels and forget-me-nots and even the vicar did not sound too convinced about the fire and brimstone elsewhere, but Stella, who only went to church to be sociable, had never seemed to believe any of it, she who had seen so much death, so many people who had not deserved to die, who always said, 'When you are dead, that's it. Dead is dead.'

'You must have heard of spiritualism.'

'Oh, but isn't all that nonsense?' Peggy said. '*That* sort of a medium; I've heard of them. Aren't they all frauds? I'm sure I've read about it – everything's done with muslin and photographs and – oh, years and years ago, in the last century, that poet, Mr Sludge – no, Robert Browning was the poet. The poem was called "Mr Sludge", he was a fake medium.'

'A lot of them are fakes,' Stella said. 'A lot of everything is faked. Banknotes, for instance. But just because a lot of banknotes are forgeries, it doesn't mean that they all are. For centuries people have believed in a life after death. Why wouldn't those who have gone there try to get in touch with the ones they've left behind. Don't you think they'd want to?'

Peggy felt uneasy and more than uneasy, because this was Stella speaking. She had always trusted Stella to be the sensible one, who solved problems, who told the truth.

'I'd have thought they'd all be too happy playing harps and singing "Holy Holy Holy" to care about the rest of us,' she said, and knew that she sounded facetious.

'Do you really believe that, the harps and the haloes?'

'No, but you don't either . . . do you?'

'There are stranger ideas. Golf courses . . .'

'In *heaven*?'

'And whisky and cigars. I don't know what the women are meant to do for eternity. Knit socks and arrange flowers, I dare say. No, Peg, there are some really peculiar theories about, put forward by the most unlikely people. But it's so hard to believe there's nothing, nothing to go to, nothing left behind, that all those millions of dead have just vanished. And they were all so young, they weren't ready to die. Oh, I know, "they were willing to lay down their lives for their country", but they weren't ready, how could they be? Some of them were not much older than you; they were so eager to fight they lied about their age. Are you ready to give your life for your country? For anything? You've hardly lived yet. It all sounded very fine – maybe they believed it before it happened, but I never saw anyone die with a smile on his face, saying, "Thank God I have done my duty." They cried for their mothers. Some had no faces—'

Stella too was crying. Peggy saw the tears in the light of the streetlamp outside. It had grown quite dark in the sitting room. She reached out and took her aunt's free hand.

'Stella, I'm sorry. I'm so sorry. I didn't mean to joke about it. Have you tried to – have you been to one of those medium things – what do they call them, séances?'

Stella nodded. Peggy could just make out the movement of her head; her cold fingers gripped Peggy's hand.

'I keep hoping he'll try to get through.'

Peggy knew what she was talking about, almost. But which 'he' did Stella mean? One of her brothers, Irene's cousin Derek, or her first fiancé, Peter? How could she ask?

'Has Irene said anything?'

'I haven't told her. She thinks I'm at meetings or out with friends when I go. She doesn't believe. She wouldn't expect to get messages from Derek. I don't know that I would. This will sound awful to you, Peggy, but I really didn't know him all that long, or all that well. We met a few times. He went back to France. He was wounded, not terribly badly but a Blighty one, enough to get him sent home. The war was nearly over, but he had to go back. They patched him up and got him fit to fight again and sent him back to die. He knew he would. I knew he would. Some men were very chivalrous to begin with, they said it wasn't fair to make a girl wait. In the end, no one was waiting. He went back the last time engaged to me but I don't think either of us expected it to last, not marriage, a lifetime together. Just those few days of leave and a promise . . .

'I never really thought Derek would try to get across.'

'Peter Heaseman? Uncle Peter?'

'We'd known each other for most of our lives,' Stella said. 'We didn't fall in love, we *were* in love, we grew into it. We shared so much, we knew everything about each other. I still miss him so dreadfully. I expect it would have been a disaster if we had married, like marrying your twin. But if anyone was going to try to reach me, it would be him. Do you see the difference?'

She could not imagine how it would feel but, yes, she could see the difference. As far as that went, she did understand.

'You go to the séances in case Peter is trying to get a message to you?'

'Yes. But nothing's ever come through.'

'Why do you have to go anywhere? Wouldn't he just try to speak to you?'

'He would if he could . . . if he's there . . . But that's what the medium's for, Peg. The go-between. Someone who's sensitive, who receives the messages and transmits them. Some people do seem to have this gift – if they can learn how to use it.'

They sat without speaking, looking past each other out of the window. Peggy watched the pillar box, people pausing to post letters through the slot; messages. At last she said, 'Do you think that's what's happening to me? That someone's trying to get in touch from the – the other side. In Morse code?'

'Peter was in Signals,' Stella said. 'And he knew you. But you say there are voices too.'

'Voices I can't understand. I'm not even sure that they *are* voices.'

'You might learn to understand them – if you were sensitive.'

'Oh!' That really was a shock. 'I might be a medium?'

'There's got to be some explanation, hasn't there? For what you're hearing.'

'But don't you think – if anyone was trying to get in touch with me – it would be Daddy?'

Stella was stealthily wiping her eyes. 'I hadn't thought of that. I'm so selfish, you must think me a pig and an idiot.' If it had been anyone else Peggy certainly would have thought so, but Stella could never be an idiot and surely someone so generous might be entitled to think of herself first, occasionally. 'Of course it could be Alan, your father. It could be anyone. Mediums can't choose who speaks to them, through them, but you'd be able to find out.'

'How?'

'We'll only do this is you want to,' Stella said. 'There's a group of people who meet together. I'm one of them.'

'Are these the interesting people – the ones you want me to meet tomorrow night? Is it going to be a séance?'

'Yes, but it's not what you think, Peggy. Perhaps I am being idiotic but I'm not so stupid as to be taken in by muslin and photographs and trumpets floating about. Fairground sideshows, and like fairground sideshows they're out to separate people from their money – but it's not like that any more. Heavens!' She stood up suddenly. 'It's so dark in here. I'm a rotten hostess, Peg. I wouldn't blame you if you never came again.'

She switched on the standard lamp in the corner. It glowed under its soft yellow shade. 'Let's sit on the divan, it's much more comfortable. Don't you love our cushions?' The divan was piled with cushions of all colours and patterns, unlike the ones at home in the parlour. There they squatted, one at each corner of chairs and sofa, brown plush or mushroom silk. The ones in the sitting room were those that had retired from the parlour, even dingier.

123

'Honestly, Peg, you wouldn't believe what some of the fakes get up to. Have you heard of ectoplasm?'

'Is it like protoplasm – I know about that from natural science. Isn't all life on earth made from it?'

'Ectoplasm's made from muslin, that's what you were reading about. It's supposed to issue from the medium – oh, don't look so scared, Peg, this is what the fakes do. It billows about and forms shapes, and faces appear; those are the photographs. You'd have to be desperate to believe it was anything supernatural. I've seen it done. It's all carried out in the dark, with eerie lights. Tables move, messages are rapped out, all done by the spirits, so-called. And yet people believe it who you think would know better.'

'Sherlock Holmes – no, Sir Arthur Conan Doyle. He does. And didn't he write that thing in the *Strand* magazine?'

'Oh, the Cottingley business, those two girls who claimed they'd photographed fairies. You or I could do that with a Kodak. Some people will believe anything.'

'I suppose it's because they want to believe,' Peggy said. 'Like the ones who get taken in by the ectoplasm stuff. Desperate.'

Stella did not answer. Curled up among the cushions at the end of the divan, she pushed a cigarette into the end of an ivory holder and lit it. The smoke coiled up into the yellow lampshade. Was that how ectoplasm looked?

'Peggy, you don't have to come with me tomorrow, and if you don't want to come I won't go off and leave you here all alone. But it's not ectoplasm, I promise. Everyone is quite ordinary and—'

'Interesting?'

'I was going to say intelligent. Not fools and dupes. The medium is a Mrs Tennant. She doesn't take money, only expenses, just her Tube fares. She just wants to help people.'

'Where will it be?'

'In a flat, not far from here. Just a drawing room; rather grander than this, though that's not difficult. And it won't be done in the dark, nothing frightening.'

'Of course I'll come,' Peggy said. 'I'm not frightened.' She did not feel happy, though. 'It's so strange, thinking that I could – well, thinking where the sounds are coming from.'

'They might not be,' Stella said. 'But there again, they might. It would be a pity not to find out. Anyway, to-morrow night is twenty-four hours away. Let's worry about this evening. Would you like an omelette for supper? I'm a dab hand at omelettes.'

Chapter 9

Lying awake later, in the bed that Irene had kindly given up, listening to Stella's quiet breathing from the other side of the strip of carpet between the beds, she wished that Stella had not mentioned twenty-four hours. A day could slip gradually away, unnoticed, but once you divided it into sections you measured its going, quarter by quarter. Somewhere near by a church clock struck. She had not expected to hear church clocks in London, only Big Ben. The bedroom, like her own at home, was at the rear of the house and faced the backs of houses in the next street. Through the half-drawn curtains she could see one window, high up, perhaps a dormer, still lighted and lonely.

The front door of the flat opened quietly. That must be Irene coming home, and it was long after midnight, almost one o'clock.

If only she could get to sleep. Tomorrow – no, today – was going to be fun. Stella had promised an expedition to the West End, to shops, and then to the theatre. 'A magical thing, we've seen it already. You'll love it.' Then out to tea and then—

Dit-dit-ditditditdit-dit-ditditdit.

Go away. Not now. She could not hum here, to drown it out, with Stella sleeping only a couple of feet away. She tried to think loudly.

What would come next, after the theatre, the magical thing? Then she remembered: the interesting people. What had she let herself in for? Hilda would have a fit, not that Hilda would approve of anything that Stella did, on principle. Mother, she was sure, would not like it. They had all seen the pictures of the Cottingley fairies and laughed at them, or rather, at the people who believed they were genuine photographs. Peggy had had her suspicions about those fairies.

In the bookcase in the parlour was a shelf of gift books, all bound in pale, smooth cloth that looked like parchment. One of them was her own, given by Grandmother Hutton for Christmas, when Peggy was still too young to enjoy much of it, although she had loved the colour plates. One of them accompanied a poem, 'A Spell for a Fairy'. When she could read the poem she was frightened by it – the spells required taking the blood of hens and 'a withered child of seven, reeking from the City slime'. She was seven. How could someone her age be withered? The girl did not look withered in the picture, only ragged. Fairies were alighting on her hand, her claw-like hand, it said in the poem. There were more fairies, in black and white, dancing across the page under the last verse. She wouldn't mind betting that those Cottingley girls had also read *Princess Mary's Gift Book*.

She lay listening to Irene creeping about in the next room and fell asleep before the church clock struck again, the Morse signals still running through her head, but much quieter, strangely, here in London. Could it be Peter Heaseman, or some other lost soul, trying to reach her with those coded messages? And if it wasn't, then who was sending them? Why?

Although she had come home so late Irene was up before them. When Peggy went into the hall she smelled fresh coffee from the kitchen where Irene, wearing a Japanese kimono instead of a dressing gown, was preparing breakfast.

'Wotcher,' she said cheerfully, waving a frying pan. 'Bacon and eggs, or are you reducing?'

'Reducing?'

'By not eating bacon and eggs. Though there's not enough of you to reduce, yet.'

'Was the meeting interesting?'

'Riotous. Nothing arouses people's passions faster than stating the bleeding obvious. Why are the poor poor? Because it suits the rich to keep them poor. The money trick – have you read *The Ragged Trousered Philanthropists*?'

'No, I haven't even heard of it.'

'That doesn't surprise me. It was written by a working man about working men, not the kind of thing young ladies are encouraged to get their hands on.'

'I've read *Pilgrim's Progress*. That was written by a working man – John Bunyan. He was a tinsmith, wasn't he?'

'Well said, but it's not a fair comparison. He wrote in the style of the King James Bible, probably the only book *he'd* ever read. And he lived in the seventeenth century, which makes him respectable. People improve enormously once they're dead.'

'No politics at this hour, please,' Stella said, looking in

through the doorway. 'We're going to be frivolous today. First stop, Gamage's, to buy a hat.'

'Haven't you got enough hats?'

'No one can have enough hats – but this one's for Peggy.'

'You don't have to buy me a hat,' Peggy said.

'Oh, but I do. And don't go all noble and say that you must live according to your means and never accept charity. I hear enough of that from Mary. If your aged auntie can't give you a present, I'd like to know who can. Anyway, I can't have you going about in that school tea cosy, feeling self-conscious. I'd be miserable for you. I'd be miserable for me; people might think I was making you wear it. Anyway, I love buying hats and as Reenie says, I have plenty. This will be an excuse.'

'Now, you must not go wild when you see the hat department,' Stella said, as they walked along Holborn. 'Hats go to people's heads.'

'Where else?' Peggy said. At that moment she would have been happy to go hatless all day. The busy street was wide, bright, windy. They strode along. She could not have walked slowly, it was the kind of day that made children skip. She was too old to skip.

'Don't be so literal. In the really smart shops they put just one dream of a hat in the window and Madame is very firm with her clients. The rest of us go to department stores and lust after the most unsuitable things. Nothing too mad for you, Peg, you'll have to wear it on the streets of Hanstead and it will have to match your coat. Otherwise you'll start hankering for a coat to live up to the hat, and shoes that match the coat – that way madness lies. Here we are.'

They stepped into a wondrous aviary of hats seemingly airborne on wings of tulle and feathers. Nearer to ground level were the sparrows and pigeons, felt hats, brown black and grey, depressingly like the one she had left in the flat.

'And nothing too extravagant or you'll feel crushed under it. No, darling, *no* artificial flowers, we'll go for style. Something stunningly simple but worn at just the right angle.'

Stella, she could see, was enjoying this as much as if she were choosing the hat for herself. She seemed to have left behind the sadness of last night, but all the women here, choosing hats, could be feeling as Stella did. Every one of them, bright and smiling as they were, might have lost someone, more than one. They could not mourn for ever, all the time. Buy a new hat and make yourself feel wonderful again, if only for a while.

'There it is,' Stella said, pointing. 'That's the one.' An assistant materialized beside them. 'Let's have it down, please.'

It was black velvet, like a tam-o'-shanter but soft and full, with a slim, dashing dart of red on one side. It fitted. Peggy looked at her reflection in the glass on the counter. There must be a catch, it was perfect. Nothing was ever perfect, not for her.

'We'll take it,' Stella said. 'No, don't wrap it up, it has to be worn this minute. It could have been designed for you alone, just the right shape for your face. Goes perfectly with your flapper and it'll look even better when you have a bob because your hair will curl.'

'I don't think Mother wants me to have a bob.'

'Oh, it'll happen sooner or later,' Stella said, as if the hair would cut itself as naturally as it had grown long. 'All over the country mothers are capitulating. Fathers hold out the longest until you point out the reduction in hairdressing bills.'

'We don't have hairdressing bills,' Peggy said. 'Mother cuts ours when it needs trimming and Hilda does hers. We have to send Ollie to the barber though. He wouldn't dare to go out in public again if it got around that his sisters cut his hair. Anyway, we'd never be able to do it properly, he'd be all over tufts and bald patches.'

'Odd, isn't it? To see him you'd think he never looked in a mirror; the same with most boys. But they're as vain as any girl on the quiet.'

The store was full of mirrors. Peggy kept seeing herself at unexpected moments and grinning helplessly because no matter how unprepared she was the hat always looked exactly right. It framed her face instead of crouching on top of her head like the school hat. It did not flop or slip.

Stella looked over her shoulder. 'You know, Peg, you're really awfully pretty – no, don't go all modest and deny it.'

'No one ever said that before, except the grannies and they have to. It's part of being a grandmother, even if the children look like trolls. Granny Hutton used to say it to Ollie until he was old enough to know what she meant.'

'Well, you've seen yourself now, so you know it's true. You wouldn't be beaming like that, otherwise. Hats really are miraculous things. Let's go and find some lunch. A lady keeps her hat on in a restaurant so you won't have to part with it yet. We'll walk on to the West End and eat, then we can take the Tube to the Regent.'

'The theatre? Isn't it in the West End? I thought they all were.'

'This one's only just become a theatre; it used to be a music hall. It's in Euston Road, opposite St Pancras Station. Have you ever seen St Pancras?'

'No. Is it special?'

'It's the cathedral of the Midland Railway. No, I'm not joking, you'll see. Every age raises great buildings to the thing it honours most. In the Middle Ages that was God, to the Victorians it was railways.'

'What about us?'

'Shopping,' Stella said. 'I ought to have taken you to Selfridges.'

If Stella had not told her that St Pancras was a railway station Peggy would have taken it for a cathedral with its turrets and spires and gothic windows. They stood outside the theatre on the far side of the road and gazed up at the great red-brick building.

'All that for a station.'

'The part we're looking at is the Grand Midland Hotel, but the train shed's just as impressive in its way. Anyway, forget marvels of nineteenth-century architecture, we're going much farther back than that.'

Peggy turned to look at the posters outside the theatre.

'*The Immortal Hour*. Is it historical, then?'

132

'What makes you think so?'

'You said it was much farther back than the last century. Immortal sounds as if something that happened a long while ago is still happening.'

'It's not historical in the 1066 sense. More ancient. It's based on the old Celtic myths of Ireland.'

'St Patrick casting out the snakes?'

'Older than that, even, the *Tuatha dé Danann*; the *Sidhe*. Fairies.'

'Oh.' Peggy knew that her face had fallen. 'A pantomime?'

'In October? No, not a pantomime, you lemon, an opera. And not that kind of a fairy, dolled-up in chiffon at three and eleven a yard. These were the grown-up kind, passionate, fierce, dangerous. It's a love story too and – oh, wait till you see it.'

Peggy was still thinking of the Cottingley fairies and the ones in *Princess Mary's Gift Book*, tiny creatures that perched on a finger like butterflies. But when they took their seats and the lights went down, and the curtain rose on a moonlit pool glimpsed among shadowy trees, she forgot the wings and the chiffon. There was music, solemn, heavy chords, a solo clarinet that rose in a sombre melody above them. From among the trees the tall figure of a man dressed in black came forward and began to sing.

> *By moon-glimmering coasts and dim grey wastes*
> *Of thistle-gathered shingle and sea-murmuring woods,*
> *Trod once but now untrod . . . under grey skies*
> *That had the grey wave sighing in their sails,*

133

Jan Mark

> *And in their drooping sails the grey sea-ebb*
> *And with the grey wind wailing evermore*
> *Blowing the dim leaf from the blackening trees,*
> *I have travelled from one darkness to another.'*

Peggy felt herself shiver, a physical thrill that seemed to begin between her thighs and surge upwards, outwards, all through her. Music had never done that before. It was all strange, unsettling; the desolate figure of the singer, Dalua, Lord of Shadow, taunted and tormented by voices from unseen singers in the wood; a beautiful woman, lost queen of a land she had forgotten; the human king who had sought perfect beauty, who had 'wooed the Immortal Hour', won the queen for himself and lost her again to the stranger who had once been her husband in the land of eternal youth and won her back with a song.

She knew that she would have understood it better if she had known the Irish myth that it was based on, but she was reminded of another myth from another place, Orpheus and Eurydice, the story of the man who so loved his wife that when she died he went down to the Underworld and, with his singing, charmed Death into giving her back to him.

Orpheus had lost his love at last as he led her back to the land of the living because he could not believe that Death would truly let her go. Here it was the human king who lost his fairy bride because no mortal could hold what lasts for ever. It was more than a lovely tragic story: no myth ever said only what it seemed to say. Men are called mortals because they die and death is the end. Orpheus could not

134

bring Eurydice back to life. The immortal fairy could not remain in the land of mortals. Those who belonged on the other side must stay there.

Afterwards it was a shock, almost painful, to come out into daylight, late afternoon sunshine, the gritty wind blowing along the Euston Road, the red-brick ramparts of St Pancras Station. The crowds who came out with them seemed equally stunned, blinking, murmuring. Stella took Peggy's arm.

'What did you think of it?'

'It was so sad, and beautiful. And the music—'

'It haunts you, doesn't it? Oh, no. Silly to say that. It hasn't had time to haunt you yet. But it will.'

Peggy was not sure that she wanted to be haunted by any more sounds, however magical and lovely, but even now it was playing itself again in her head. It was the first time she had heard a harp, but she knew that song of enchantment already.

'Did you say you'd seen it before?'

'Twice. We went last week when it opened, but I managed to catch it two years ago – it was on for a few days at the Old Vic. I'd been longing for another chance. I may go again. It's only a shilling if you sit in the gallery.'

'Three times! Do you love it so much?'

'Don't you?'

She could not disappoint Stella. '*Oh, yes*.' But she did not think she wanted to see it, hear it again so soon. If the music did return to haunt her she would be able to hear it whenever she chose, the harp, the high, heartless singing of the unseen fairies, voices in the air. Yes, it was lovely, magical, but her own heart was with the king who lost his love and his dream . . . Where had she heard that before, that to possess the dream was to destroy it?

'We've done unforgiveable things to the fairies,' Stella was saying. 'Miniatured them like lapdogs, turned them into harmless domestic pets. We keep them at the bottom of the garden.'

'I suppose they're easier to handle when they're small,' Peggy said.

'We're afraid of what we can't handle.' Almost inaudible among the traffic Stella sang quietly, '*How beautiful they are, the lordly ones, who dwell in the hills, in the hollow hills* . . . You know what the hollow hills are, don't you? Tumuli, barrows, burial mounds. All those tales of putting out bread and milk for the fairies – people were terrified of them. They blighted your crops, lamed your cattle, stole your children. What could you do but placate them, creatures who did not know human pity? They were unknowable. People have always feared the unknowable.'

It was easy to talk about, walking along the city street towards Marylebone. The unknowable was not here in the sunshine and bustle, it was in the shadows and silence. *I have travelled from one darkness to another.* To what darkness would she be travelling tonight?

Chapter 10

Stella and Irene lived in a house that had been sliced up like a loaf into flats. Devonshire Mansions was a whole block, especially built. It had an electric lift which carried them to the third floor. The uniformed maid who answered the door and took their coats and gloves recognized Stella and called her Miss Holt. Peggy was afraid that she would have to give up her hat, but Stella made no move to take off her own so she was able to keep it. She felt confident under that hat.

They were shown into a room which would have held the whole of Stella's flat and another one besides. Heavy red-velvet curtains hung in the bay window at one end, making it seem as wide as the stage at the Regent. In front of them chairs were arranged around a huge oval table. At the other end, on thick carpets, were sofas and easy chairs around a bright fire burning in a grate surrounded by as much marble as the British Museum. There were real oil paintings, not prints, hanging on the walls in heavy gilt frames.

'Miss Holt, Miss Hutton,' the maid said, announcing them, and went away to answer the doorbell.

A tall, white-haired woman came towards them from among a group of people who were standing talking quietly. She was plainly dressed but even Peggy could see how well tailored her costume was, how expensive the material. Everyone was well dressed, not in evening clothes but in the next best thing. It was not quite like a funeral but there was that same feeling of reverence, reverent seriousness, that hung over funerals; the funerals of old people who had died in the fullness of years.

After all, Peggy thought, we are here to meet the dead; and then wondered if perhaps that was not an irreverent thing to think. Stella had promised, no muslin, no ectoplasm; they were not going to meet the dead. But if things went well the dead might speak to them.

And no table rapping. Who was it who rapped on her skull instead, vainly sending out his coded signals that only she could hear, and could not read?

If things went well? Did she want to hear the dead speaking? Did she want to hear anything at all from the dead? Was she hearing from them already? Did she really believe that her Morse code messages were coming from the other side?

'This is my niece, Peggy,' Stella said, introducing her to the woman who had come to greet them. 'Peggy, this is our hostess, Lady Mallett.'

Lady Mallett. Ought she to curtsy? But Lady Mallett was simply holding out her hand.

'You're very welcome, my dear.' Someone else spoke to Stella and Lady Mallett guided Peggy gently towards the group with an arm about her shoulders. 'Your aunt tells me that you too may be sensitive. Is that so?'

Stella had been talking about her. Did she feel betrayed? No, not betrayed, not to this kindly woman who reminded her of Granny Hutton, but even so . . . she had *confided* in Stella.

'I don't know, yet,' she said, weakly.

'If you are, I hope it brings you much happiness,' Lady Mallett said. 'Because, if you have the gift it can bring much happiness to others. Above all, don't be afraid of it. When you meet Mrs Tennant I think you'll see that there's nothing to be afraid of.'

'Is she here – Mrs Tennant?'

'Yes, but she's resting just now. She finds it very tiring. She's not a young thing like you.'

'Tiring? What happens?'

'Don't look so alarmed. I dare say you've heard strange things about séances but we don't even think of our evening meetings here as séances. Nothing alarming will happen, I promise. Didn't Miss Holt explain to you?'

'Yes, but you said it was tiring. I just wondered . . .'

'What Mrs Tennant does for us requires a great deal of concentration, expense of spiritual energy. She gives of herself unstintingly – oh, do excuse me for a moment.'

Another visitor was being announced. As Lady Mallett turned away Peggy took the opportunity to find a seat in the corner where no one would notice her. There were about fifteen people in the room now, talking to one another in hushed voices. Most of them were Mother's age or older; there were several white heads. Stella was talking to a man and woman who looked quite young.

Peggy noticed then that almost half the people there were men. For some reason she had thought that séances were things that only women went to – except for

Robert Browning, and he had decided that once was enough. And there had been as many men as women in the theatre this afternoon, to see *The Immortal Hour,* the play about fairies. Sir Arthur Conan Doyle had written the article about fairies. Weren't men supposed to despise such things? What would Ollie make of it, with his books about gorilla hunters, intrepid explorers and Zulu warriors?

Stella noticed her, said something to the young couple, and came over.

'You look as though you were hiding from the grown-ups, tucked away there.'

'I'm just watching,' Peggy said.

'That must be exciting. Ah, we're going to sit down now.'

Peggy was already sitting but everyone else, as if at a signal that she had missed, began moving towards the long table at the other end of the room. Reluctantly she stood up and let Stella lead her to one of the empty chairs, and they sat next to each other at the foot of the table, facing a big carver which stood empty at the opposite end. No one sat in that. Although this table was oval Peggy thought of King Arthur with his round one, a place at it for every knight; and the Siege Perilous, the empty chair where no one might sit until the knight for whom it was intended came among them.

When everyone was seated someone came into the room and Lady Mallett ushered her to the table, where she sat down in the Siege Perilous.

'Good evening, friends,' she said, and everyone answered, 'Good evening.' Peggy was reminded of the

Ladies' Benevolent Circle, which was run by the vicar's wife and raised money for good works. Mrs Tennant could easily have been a vicar's wife, dressed in a plain brown coat and hat, plain face, brown hair drawn back in a bun. Now that she was seeing a real medium she knew that she had been picturing veils, beads, oriental drapery and a crystal ball; dark, eastern eyes, a husky foreign voice and a tang of exotic perfume.

Mrs Tennant's voice was very pleasant – what would it be like when the spirits spoke through her? But as soon as she began speaking Peggy knew that Hilda would say that she wasn't out of the top drawer. Still, if Lady Mallett, who obviously was out of the top drawer, was happy to have her sitting at her table, she must be the right sort.

Why *were* they sitting around a table? Would they have to hold hands? She was happy to hold Stella's hand on her left, but on her right was a thin, sombre man who did not look as if he ever held hands with anyone. No, people were keeping their hands on their laps or folded on the table. Was the table going to move? Would the spirits rap on it? At the other end of the room the maid was putting out the lights until they were left with one softly glowing lamp behind Mrs Tennant.

There was something lying on the table in front of the woman – hands? Where had they come from? No, not hands, gloves; there must be one from every person in the room – there was Stella's blue velvet. Why? Who had said that this stranger might have Peggy's glove? Stella? It was very quiet. She could hear someone breathing and then – *ditditdit-dit-dit-dit-ditditditditditdit* –

Not *now*, she begged silently. I don't want to get messages. *No*. Don't send messages to me.

'Tom's here,' Mrs Tennant said suddenly. 'Most of you know Tom, but if it's your first time I have to warn you – you mustn't mind what he says. He was a very ordinary lad, not educated. He died of influenza and he never had much schooling.'

She might have been talking about a real person who had just walked in, but all the while she was speaking she was gently moving her hands along the row of gloves until she paused and took hold of one. 'Now, Tom says, Robert's with him. Robert. Is anyone hoping to hear from Robert? He popped off in 'seventeen – no, don't laugh. Tom doesn't know any better. Robert wants to talk to Mag . . . Meg. Meggie? Is there a Margaret here?'

Peggy flinched and felt Stella's hand on her arm. It couldn't be for her. She didn't know anyone called Robert – did she?

Someone further round the table said, 'I'm Margaret. Is that Robin?' A woman, her voice shaking. 'Is that my Robin?'

'He says . . . Meg was the only one who ever called him Robin. You're not to worry any more. He's very happy where he is, not what he was expecting, all calm and peaceful – but that doesn't mean they don't have a bit of a laugh now and again. He sends his love to Mildred – no, sorry. Do pay attention, Tom. Mildred's there with him, tell her to wait, Tom. It's not Mildred; Milly. Millicent.'

'Yes,' the woman sighed. 'Millicent, his cousin.'

'She's to be happy, and keep on keeping on. There'll be

good news for her soon and a great happiness; the sort that lasts.'

'Oh, what—?'

'No, he's going now, Tom says. That's all.'

'Oh, *thank* you,' the woman called Meg whispered.

'Who's that? Alfred? Tom says he's got an Alfred for us. Does anyone . . . ? Are you sure, Tom?'

The stern-looking man beside Peggy half raised a hand. 'I'm Alfred.'

'Don't be saucy, Tom,' Mrs Tennant said. 'He says I ought to listen more carefully. Message *for* Alfred, from Jack . . . James? Jack.'

'Yes,' the man said. Peggy could not think of him as Alfred. He looked like a bishop. Perhaps he was. 'My son Jack. Is that really you, my boy?'

'Now, slow down, Tom.' Mrs Tennant looked a little to one side when she spoke to Tom. Could she *see* him? And cocked her head slightly afterwards, as if listening. Could she hear him? 'If you didn't gabble so, we wouldn't have these muddles. Tom says Jack's been waiting, ever so long. He got proper browned off, Tom says. But it's all right now you're here. You shouldn't ought to have left it so long, making yourself miserable, when Jack was here all the time, twiddling his thumbs while you made up your mind. But not to worry, he says. Better late than never. Now you've made your mind up to believe, he'll always be near you, looking out for you. He's happy now, he says. Mind you keep happy too, there's nothing to be miserable about. When your time comes he'll be ready to meet you.'

'Jack, wait—'

'No more now,' Mrs Tennant said. 'It's getting busy. Alice – is Alice here? Alice, it's your pal Lydia what went over in the Zeppelin raid . . .'

And on it went, like a telephone exchange: Lydia for Alice, Gerald for Agnes; William kept butting in asking for Wilfred, but there was no Wilfred at the table; Mildred again, for Hubert. No one came through for Stella, no one, to her great relief, for Peggy. It was true, as Lady Mallett had said, that there was nothing alarming about Mrs Tennant, sitting at the end of the table, chatting to Tom, and nothing alarming about Tom, either, although none of them could see him or hear him. You had to like Tom, who was perfectly at his ease and no respector of persons. The Alice whose pal Lydia had come through was Lady Mallett herself, who surely had never talked about having a pal in her life. Sitting there, listening to Mrs Tennant relaying Tom's messages, it was so natural to believe that she really was talking to him, that he actually was in the room with them. And he was getting the names right most of the time although the messages were all very vague, mainly about being happy. That was what people wanted to be told, wasn't it? That the friends and relatives they had lost were happy.

The words were tailing off, pauses lengthening, no one left but William, still trying to get Wilfred, who wasn't there.

'Tom's off now,' Mrs Tennant said. 'He's getting tired. That's all right, Tom, you've done us proud. Thank you, dear.'

She relaxed and faced them for the first time, smiling

and tranquil. All round the table faces smiled back; there were little murmurs of thanks. Some people wept quietly but not sadly. The man beside Peggy, Alfred, wiped his eyes as the maid came in and turned on the lights.

'Don't be disappointed if you didn't get a message,' Mrs Tennant said. 'It can take time. It took a while for some of you to pluck up the courage to come along here, didn't it?' She was looking at Alfred. 'Well, it's the same on the other side. Some of them are a bit confused, I dare say. Maybe they don't quite like to try, or they tried and didn't get anywhere the first time, like poor old William. Let's pray that his friend Wilfred is guided to someone who'll be able to put him through. We'll just have a little private prayer before we go, shall we? Remember Wilfred in your prayers.'

As if they were in church. Peggy, recalling Miss Kelsey's fulminations, had a feeling that the Church did not approve of what had been going on here this evening and would have made heretics of these sorrowful, hopeful people, and kindly Mrs Tennant and her Tom who would not, Peggy imagined, give two hoots about what the Church thought. They all bowed their heads. In the silence she could hear the Morse code again, then it stopped and as the group around the table was beginning to stir and stand up she caught the twanging words that were not quite words. Then the sounds were immersed in other sounds.

Peggy was turning to Stella when Mrs Tennant caught her eye and beckoned.

Stella noticed. 'Go and speak to her,' she said. She was still sitting, not weeping but looking blank, refusing to let something show. Peggy had forgotten how much she too must have been hoping for a message, like William on the other side with a message and no one to give it to. Mrs Tennant was nodding and smiling and the group had now moved away to the other end of the room, where refreshments were being served, just like at the Ladies' Benevolent, although several of the guests were leaving, eager to be alone with their joy, or their sorrow.

'You're the young lady who hears things?' Mrs Tennant said. She took Peggy's hand and so felt her jolt of shock. 'Oh, don't worry, I'm not seeing into your head, or your heart.'

'How did you know?'

'Your age. Most of the others here could give you thirty years at least. But I could tell you weren't very happy to be here. Nothing strange about that, dear. Anyone would have noticed who didn't have other things on their minds. You're thinking this is something you don't much want to be mixed up in, aren't you? I don't blame you. I wouldn't have cared for it much at your age. How old are you, sixteen?'

'Fourteen. You weren't always . . . weren't born . . . ?'

'Well, I must have been, but I didn't know about it until a few years back.' Mrs Tennant talked as if being a medium was the most ordinary thing in the world, like being a dentist, or a librarian. 'What makes you think you might be?'

'I don't,' Peggy said.

'No, I don't either.' Mrs Tennant still held her hand and squeezed it. 'It's nothing to be afraid of, believe me, but who's been putting ideas into your head?'

'My Aunt Stella. She didn't put ideas into my head, I think she's just hoping. Tom didn't have a message for her. I saw you pick up her glove twice, but nothing happened. It's just that lately I've been hearing things; it sounds like Morse code and sometimes, I think, voices – but I can never make out what they say. Not like Tom. Can you really *hear* Tom?'

'Not the way I'm hearing you,' Mrs Tennant said, frankly. 'It's more like I can feel what he says. I don't try to explain it. I don't know where your Morse code's coming from, dear, but I don't think it's the other side. Poor things, they do so want to get through. I can't imagine they'd make it any more difficult for themselves than it is already. 'Course, you might get some Clever Dick trying to show off his word speed, but I don't think it's very likely, do you? Most of them have left off being clever.'

'What about the voices?'

'If they are voices. Had you thought of getting your ears syringed? I'm told that can make a world of difference. My sister thought she was going deaf for years and then she got a new young doctor. "Wax," he said, and it was.'

Peggy felt herself smiling back at Mrs Tennant.

'You think I ought to have my mind on higher things,' Mrs Tennant said. 'I'm nothing special, I've just got a special gift. Maybe that's why Tom talks to me. He wouldn't have the nerve to be control for anybody grand. Now, dear, if there's someone like Tom trying to get through to you, you'll know all about it. They *will* get through, you won't be able to ignore it. But if there isn't, all the trying in the world won't make it happen. And that can lead to trouble, fakery, a lot of dangerous nonsense.'

'Ectoplasm?'

'And that. Worse. You're a sensible girl, I can see that, too. Stop worrying. I know you don't want to disappoint your auntie but you follow your own nose.'

Lady Mallett was hovering. Peggy shook hands with Mrs Tennant and went to join Stella.

'Ready to go?' Stella said. 'Or do you want to stay for coffee?'

'Let's go,' Peggy said. 'It's awfully warm in here.'

They said goodbye. The maid fetched their coats. The gloves were laid out on a marble-topped table in the hall, where someone had reunited them with their other halves.

Out in the street Stella tucked Peggy's arm into her own.

'That wasn't so terrifying, was it?'

'Not a bit.' But it had been disturbing, until the end. 'I'm sorry there was nothing for you.'

'Oh, I keep hoping,' Stella said. 'But what were you talking about with the medium?'

'She knew about me. Did you tell her?'

'No – it must have been Lady Mallett. Oh, how things do get passed around. Did you think I'd been gossiping about you?'

'How did Lady Mallett know?'

'I only asked her if I might bring you along because there was a chance you might be sensitive too. I didn't go into details. What did Mrs Tennant say?'

Peggy decided not to mention the medium's advice about ear wax. 'She was very kind. She asked me what I heard . . . and she said she didn't think it sounded as if it

148

was coming from the other side. I did like her awfully, Stella. And she warned me – she said that if I wasn't sensitive all the trying in the world wouldn't make me. That if I was I'd know soon enough, but if I wasn't, it would be dangerous to try.'

'That puts me in my place, doesn't it?' Stella said, quietly. 'You must think I'm every kind of fool.'

'No, never. Of course I don't. I just didn't realize how sad you were. You never show it.' She hugged Stella's elbow. They were walking along dark, empty pavements from one oasis of light to the next, past warmly lit windows in the tall houses on either side; where you could look down over area railings into basement kitchens. Sometimes a servant glanced up from a table or a sink. It was not very cold but there was rain in the wind. Peggy shrugged herself deeper into the long scarf that Stella had lent her, warm in the lovely new hat that Stella had given her.

'This is just what I thought London would be like. This is what I dream of: my own flat, working at the thing I like most, going where I like, when I like, being with the people I like most.'

'I'm still one of them, then?'

'Of course. You always will be.'

'What are you going to tell them at home?'

'That we went to the opera, and had lunch in a restaurant in Oxford Street and you bought me a beautiful hat and we visited a friend of yours called Lady Mallett. That will make Hilda absolutely sick with envy.'

'The hat? Don't flaunt it.'

'It's not really flauntable, is it? Just splendid. No, having met a lady in her own home. They always trot out a Lady on Speech Day to hand out the prizes and some of them are real Aunt Sallies. At least they don't give the speeches. And every year there's this sort of contest for the one who'll be chosen to hand over the bouquet – to the Lady. The prefects do it; first they tot up all the order marks and conduct marks and deduct them from the Commendations you've got – if you've got any – and then they work out from that the most worthy person to do the presentation. You have to wear a special sash, and curtsy, but it's a swindle. They choose from a different year each time, but it always goes to some simpering goody-goody, no one who's really nice or clever.'

'They never choose you, then.'

'Not likely, especially now. Hilda's a sub-pre. No, I was thinking of Vera Openshaw, she left last year. She won heaps of prizes and everyone liked her and she had topping good looks, but she never got chosen. Though knowing Vera,' Peggy said thoughtfully, 'she'd probably have turned it down on principle. That would have been a scandal. I don't think she approved of the aristocracy.'

'Lady Mallett's no aristocrat.' Stella laughed. 'Her husband's one of Lloyd George's life peers. It's all political manoeuvring. Do you and Hilda get on so very badly?'

'What's really annoying,' Peggy said, 'is that there's no need. Mother never finds fault and that's not because she's easy-going. I do my share of the housework, I do my schoolwork. I don't bring the family into disrepute.'

'Except over that silly friend of yours – Dorothy, wasn't it? I meant to ask you about that. Are you still friends?'

'No. She avoids me like the plague. Sits next to someone else in form, walks with someone else in crocs, goes home a different way.'

'Her loss.'

'She doesn't look very happy. But Marjorie, a girl in my form, said that everyone's noticed – well, they couldn't help noticing – and that they'll start taking sides. I said there was no need for that, it was private, and she said it wouldn't happen on purpose, it would just happen. After all, *she's* on my side.'

'Good for Marjorie. Are you friends?'

'We weren't, particularly, but that wasn't why. She came right out and asked me what had happened, so I told her, and she thought I'd done the right thing – telling Dorothy, I mean.' The rest of their conversation came back to her. 'Stella, what's a White Slaver?'

'What on earth made you think of that?'

'We were talking about it – me and Marjorie. But it was something Mother let slip and then she got embarrassed and said to ask you.'

'Why does she think I have all the answers? How much have I got to explain? Do you know what a prostitute is?'

'Yes, a bad woman. I read it somewhere.'

'Not at school, I bet, unless it was in the Bible. "And Rahab was an harlot." I wouldn't use the term "bad woman". There's nothing bad about being a prostitute, if that's what you want to be. Or even if you don't – plenty of perfectly nice women turn to selling themselves because it's their only way to learn a living. But a White Slaver's a pimp, worse. Traps a woman into prostitution and takes her earnings. Sometimes she's shipped abroad with no way of getting back.'

'Why White?'

'A woman in that situation is a slave, isn't she? The original slaves came from Africa. Some say marriage is a form of prostitution – no, don't let's go into that. What *were* we talking about to get on to this?'

'Hilda. Why we don't get on. Why she nags all the time. She even picks on me at school.'

'Perhaps she's trying to be impartial, afraid of being accused of favouritism.'

'Fat chance. Who'd accuse her of favouritism at home?'

'Some people,' Stella said, 'can only value themselves by believing that everyone else is a knave or a fool. Look at Christians – naturally they think that their religion is the right one, of course they do, otherwise they'd be something else, Muslims or Buddhists, who, of course, think *their* religion is the right one. And then they all divide themselves into denominations and sects, and tell themselves that there is only one way to be a Christian, *their* way, and everybody else is wrong. At least they've left off setting fire to each other – for the time being. Just think of the God of Love, Peg, up there, leaning over the edge and watching his believers massacre the opposition. At least atheists don't go to war for the right to be atheists and convert the devout. After all, basically, there's only one way to be an atheist.'

'The Bolsheviks are atheists, aren't they? Miss Kelsey says they are.'

'Oh, Peggy, you think too fast. Yes, they are, but they

didn't overthrow the Tsar to save themselves the bother of going to church.'

'Here's your pillar box,' Peggy said, as they came to the corner of Stella's street. 'Don't you feel happy when you see it? *Your* pillar box. *Your* home.'

'Don't you feel that when you see your front door?'

'It's not the same. It's where I live, but it's not *my* home. It's a house and I'm in it. When I have a home it'll be somewhere I've chosen, somewhere I've made my own.'

Chapter 11

'Ted said he might look in today,' Irene remarked at breakfast.

'Will you wait in for him?' Stella said.

'Oh yes. It would be a pity if no one were here. You two will be going out, won't you?'

'I've got to go and see that damp dishtowel of a woman in Pimlico, the one who wants me to tutor her daughter. It's an act of charity.'

'Won't she pay you?' Peggy asked.

'Through the nose, you bet. But Cecily's bright and clever. If she gets into Cambridge it'll be her one chance of escape, otherwise her days'll be spent waiting for a husband and winding Mama's wool. Mama can only see a plain girl in glasses with pretty sisters who'll marry first. Is Brian coming with Ted?'

'Probably, he never turns down the chance of a ride in the motor. Why don't you stay here, Peggy? You all got on like a house on fire, last time, and you don't want to trail over to Pimlico.'

'Good idea,' Stella said. 'I'll be back for lunch, anyway. If you decide to go out, ring me at Mrs Cowley's and I'll meet you somewhere. That suit you, Peg?'

Peggy nodded. She did not feel like going anywhere, not yet. She had slept badly, the Morse had been more penetrating than ever, coming in bursts, and she had been kept awake too by the thought of the evening at Lady Mallett's, of Mrs Tennant and her Tom. She did not want a Tom of her own and from what the medium had said, she was unlikely to have one, but she was no closer to knowing where the signals came from. And her tooth had been aching again. When she got home she would have to pluck up the courage to tell Mother, and make another appointment with the Highland Butcher.

Stella went out. Peggy washed up the breakfast things and sprawled on the divan to read the Sunday paper, a luxury they never had at home, while Irene sat writing at the table in the window. It was quiet, but not so quiet that she could hear the signals. Traffic went by, somewhere close a barrel organ was playing, the same tune over and over again, as annoying in its way as the Morse, but gradually becoming more distant. When the doorbell rang they both jumped.

'Run down and answer it, there's an angel,' Irene said, without looking up. 'If I lose the thread of this . . .'

Peggy went down the two flights to the hall, past doors where voices could be heard or a gramophone played. How odd to have all these other people living in the same house, who never met. She opened the heavy front door and there were Ted and Brian on the step, the Morris gleaming at the kerbside behind them, in the sunshine. They looked surprised to see her then, she couldn't help noticing, pleased.

'Oh, ripping,' Brian said. 'I didn't know you'd be here.'

'Are the girls at home?' Ted asked.

'Irene is. Stella had to go out. Oh, do come up,' Peggy said. 'Better go in quietly. She's in the middle of writing something fearfully important and she doesn't want to lose the thread.'

'I told her we were coming,' Ted complained as they reached the door of the flat. Peggy had left it open.

'I heard that,' Irene called. 'You said you *might* come. Was I supposed to sit here and pick at my embroidery, ready to leap up if you decided to drop by?'

'No, you kept Peggy on hand for that,' Ted said.

'Oh, go boil your head,' his sister said. 'I just didn't want to break off in the middle of a sentence. You all know where the coffee is.'

'I'll make it,' Peggy said. The room seemed to shrink around them with Ted and Brian in it, not so much tall as big, and Brian still growing. He was already shaving, she noticed. Ted sat down and swiped the *Sunday Pictorial* but Brian followed her into the kitchen.

'It's jolly here, isn't it?' he said. 'Like a doll's house.'

'You don't mean Stella and Irene are dolls, I hope.' Peggy lit the gas under the kettle. 'Or did you mean they're just playing at keeping house?'

'Don't get prickly – it's all scaled down, like a model, really. The family pile is huge and gloomy and the furniture's like something archaeologists find in a tomb. I guess Reenie likes to have things small.'

'Where is it? The coffee's in that can up there.'

'The one that's got COFFEE stencilled on it? We live outside Chelmsford, in Essex. It's the ancestral home, but for Ted it's just the best place to be. He works for Marconi.'

156

'The telegraph man?'

'Wireless telephony,' Brian said. He looked doubtful. 'Are girls interested in that kind of thing?'

'You're as bad as Ollie. Women have been operating telegraph offices since they were first invented. And the telephones. I suppose they must be interested. Of course, they *might* prefer barbola work.'

'Sorry, but they really aren't doing wireless telephony yet. No reason why they shouldn't, though.'

'This wireless telephony, explain it. I know about the telegraph, we've got the wires at the end of the garden – you saw them. All along the railway line.'

'With wireless telegraphy you – well, obviously, you haven't got the wires. That's how they get in touch with ships. There aren't any telegraph wires out in the Atlantic, are there? They can't send down a line and hook up with the Cable. Remember the *Titanic*? After that they had to have a twenty-four-hour radio watch on all big ships. In 1913 the *Volturno* caught fire in mid-Atlantic and ten ships went to the rescue. They'd picked up the distress signals.'

'Yes, but how's it done?'

'The signal's sent along electromagnetic waves instead of wires. That's why it's wire*less*.'

'Why's it called radio, then?'

'Because the waves radiate, in all directions. With a wire you can only go from point to point. The signal goes where the wire goes.'

'The telegraph.'

'Forget the telegraph, it's old hat. Telephones use wires too. But what people have been working on for, oh, twenty years, longer, is transmitting sound as well as signals, on carrier waves. Marconi wasn't the first but he's always been out in front.'

'Sounds . . . ? Voices?'

'Yes, sounds over distance. That's what telephone means. Don't you do Greek?'

'I can start in the Sixth if I want to,' Peggy said. 'So, Marconi's invented a telephone that doesn't need wires.'

'It's not a telephone, it's radio. There are hundreds of people with receiving sets, picking up transmissions, but of course Ted's got a transmitter as well. He had to get a licence from the Post Office but that wasn't difficult, not with his training. We bribed the vicar to confirm that he was a person of good character—'

'Transmitter? How does it work? I pick up a telephone and the call gets through on waves instead of wires?'

'Yes, but it's *not* a telephone system, you're not making a call. It's a broadcast. Hey, let the kettle go off the boil. You should never make coffee with boiling water.'

'Why not?'

'It tastes like burnt rubber. And it makes the milk go oily.'

'That must be why ours is always so foul. I didn't know *boys* were interested in things like that.'

'Quits,' Brian said. 'Pour it now. No, it won't be like a telephone. There'll be one place with a powerful transmitter putting out – oh, say a concert or a lecture, broadcasting it. Like sowing seeds in a field, you don't plant them one at a time in rows, do you? You walk along throwing them from one side to the other, that's broadcasting. A radio broadcast's the same idea. Electromagnetic waves go everywhere, they have to, like light, carrying music, talk, anything, any sound. Anything that can be heard can be broadcast.'

'And how do you receive it?' Peggy put the lid on the coffee pot and set the kettle back on the stove. 'You said a set.'

'A receiving set, valves, or crystals, though with valves you need an aerial and a mast – you must have seen them, even in Hanstead. There's probably one in the next street. Everyone will have them soon, when the BBC starts broadcasting.'

'BBC?'

'British Broadcasting Company. Marconi's have been transmitting weather reports in Morse from Cornwall for a couple of years now. At Chelmsford Ted's been putting out speech and music on two seven fifty metres, but at Writtle—'

'On what?'

'Two thousand seven hundred and fifty metres, the length of the wave. We're not the only ones. The Americans are way ahead, of course, and the Dutch have been broadcasting concerts. It's nothing new. They've been transmitting time signals from the Eiffel Tower since before the war. I say, it's awful you don't know any of this. It's in all the papers. Why, Essenden managed to send speech and music on eighty kilohertz back in 1906. He sang Christmas carols.'

'Kilohertz?'

'Hertz, named after . . . Hertz. Electricity's the thing to

be in if you want to be immortal. Things get named after you – well, better than that, your name becomes the thing. Watts – James Watt, you know, the inventor. Farads – after Michael Faraday, Hertz, Amps – that's Ampère, Volts from Volta . . . Röntgen and Curie – that's radioactivity, of course. X-rays. You know about *them*.'

She did, just. In a couple of minutes Brian Summersby had managed to introduce her not only to things she knew nothing about but to things she had not known she knew nothing about. One item stood out, a fact she ought to have known, probably had known if she'd thought about it: sound did not need to travel along wires in order to cover long distances. The air was full of it, signals, speech, music, carried in all directions, *broadcast*; all you had to do was reach up, as if picking a quince, and pluck it down.

'How do those receivers work?'

Ted put his head round the door. 'Where's the coffee, you burbling jabberwock?'

'Ladies present.'

'The lady knows I mean you.' He began taking down cups and saucers. 'Milk jug. Sugar bowl. *Spoons*.'

'Stop hectoring,' Brian said amiably. If only she could turn such sunny indifference on Hilda's nagging – no, hectoring. Splendid word. But Ted was doing it in fun and Brian knew it. Easy to be sunny, these two liked each other, friends as well as brothers.

'Brian was explaining about wireless telephony,' Peggy said.

'Didn't know the oaf could even spell it. You must be frightfully interested, I don't think.'

'Oh, but I am,' Peggy said. 'I want to know how the receivers work.'

'Thinking of getting one?'

She wondered if she dared to tell him that, mysteriously, she seemed to have one already. 'No, but it *is* frightfully interesting. All that sound out there – in here – how do you *get* it?'

'You could build a crystal set,' Ted said, taking her literally. 'A valve receiver would set you back about fourteen guineas, and of course you'd need the aerial. But don't rush into it, everything's developing so fast. There's going to be an amalgamation of all the wireless companies—'

'The BBC?'

He nodded approvingly, not knowing that Brian had just told her. '—putting out regular programmes. As soon as it becomes popular, and it will, prices will come down. The BBC will be on the air in a few weeks.'

He carried the tray into the sitting room. Brian followed with the coffee pot. Peggy took down the biscuit barrel, checked to see if it contained enough for four and went after them. She still did not know how receiving sets worked – valves? Crystals? Aerials? But something was clearer anyhow. Those invisible radio waves, named after Mr Hertz – probably Herr Hertz – were everywhere, not travelling along wires but rolling free through the atmosphere, like light itself. Suddenly, the fact that she could hear what they were carrying was not so unnerving, a lot less unnerving than getting messages from the other side via Mrs Tennant's Tom.

These messages might not be for her at all. If they were being broadcast, anyone could pick them up.

161

She noticed that her tooth had stopped aching.

She was back in Hanstead by eight. Walking up Gladstone Road she passed the pillar box and thought of the one on the corner of Stella's street in Marylebone. It did not have the same effect and no, the sight of her own front door did not fill her with happy excitement.

They were all in the kitchen playing Newmarket Steeplechase on the table, so loudly that they did not hear her come in. The set they had came with model lead horses and it was a family tradition to make as much row as possible as they galloped round the board. Under years of this bashing the little lead legs had curled up so that they looked like rocking horses. Even Hilda joined in but she was facing the door to the hall and stopped in mid-shout as Peggy opened it.

'You've missed supper,' she said.

Peggy thought of all the nice people she had spent the day with. She thought of Brian and Ted.

'Stop hectoring,' she said. 'Why don't you say what you really think. Let yourself go. "Oh, Peggy, how lovely to see you back safe and sound. I thought you'd been seized by White Slavers."'

'What's White Slavers?' Ollie said.

'Don't be disgusting,' Hilda said. 'Where do you pick up these awful expressions.'

Peggy caught her mother's eye.

'She picked that one up from me, dear,' Mother said. 'We didn't wait supper but I'll make you scrambled eggs, shall I?'

'I'll do it, but I'm not sure that I want much. We had a simply enormous lunch – at a curry restaurant; real Indian waiters. And I had a bun on the train.'

'You enjoyed yourself, then.'

'It was glorious. We went to the theatre – an opera, and Stella bought me a hat, look.'

'I suppose you lost yours,' Hilda said. 'Do pay attention, Ollie, it's your throw.'

'No, I didn't lose it but it would have looked awfully odd in London, on a weekend. It just shrieks *school hat!* Don't you think this one's lovely?'

'It won't look like that for long,' Hilda said. 'And who were those interesting people you were going to meet?'

All at once she felt sorry for Hilda who, she saw, was madly envious, and she remembered Stella's warning: *Don't flaunt.* If only Hilda weren't so disapproving of Stella and Irene she might have been the one who had spent the weekend in London and eaten real Indian food and seen *The Immortal Hour.*

Or perhaps not. Hilda hadn't been hearing things, and Stella was about as fond of Hilda as Hilda was of Stella. She decided not to say, as she had planned to, 'Oh, and we paid a call on Lady Mallett.' In any case, she did not want to trap herself into saying anything that might give away what had happened at Lady Mallett's. Mother, she knew, thought that spiritualists were meddling with dark forces and Hilda would disapprove of them because she was Hilda and they were just one more thing to disapprove of.

'Where did you sleep?' Hilda asked, curiously.

'In the bath – no, of course I didn't. Irene gave up her bed.'

'They've got two, then?'

'Two what?'

'Beds.'

'And a divan. Why——?'

Mother chimed in. 'Go and unpack, darling, and I'll make us all some tea.'

'And then I'll tell you about *The Immortal Hour*, the opera we saw.'

She could still remember that song, even some of the words. Tomorrow she would try to get the harp accompaniment on the piano, although it would not sound the same as the harp that had played in the theatre, that eerie, rippling rhythm. She could hear it now, in her head.

Later, in bed, she played it over and over again: *How beautiful they are, the lordly ones . . .*

Then the Morse started up, just as she was falling asleep. She was annoyed, but this time she was not particularly worried. All over the country, in Europe, across the Atlantic, the air was humming with Herr Hertz's electromagnetic waves, transmitted by people like Ted Summersby, listened to by people like Maurice Hendry. And by some wonderful chance she, Peggy Hutton of 39 Gladstone Road, Hanstead, could hear them, without a receiving set. She too had a special gift, not dubious and supernatural like Mrs Tennant's, but modern and technical. Why hadn't she told Brian about it? Brian had spoken eagerly of miracles to come, of talking pictures, television, but he had said nothing about people picking up Hertzian waves in their heads. He might have found the idea fascinating – conversely he might have thought that she was just making it up, trying to appear interesting, and then he would despise her.

She was glad she had said nothing. She liked Brian. Brian liked her. She wanted him to go on liking her. If he thought she was spooky he might change his mind.

Ollie was hovering at the gate on Monday morning, instead of hurrying on ahead before the shameful existence of his sisters was revealed to passing friends. To Peggy's surprise he fell into step beside her, not even pretending that he just happened to be going in the same direction.

Peggy was about to say, 'What are you after?' when she realized that she would sound just like Hilda, but they passed the pillar box and Ollie still had not said anything. Could there be something bothering him that he was afraid or embarrassed to mention? He had never actually said anything about the bullying, leaving her to make her own deductions. She ought to give him a leg up.

'See any good engines on Friday?'

'Engines?' His thoughts were not on trains.

'At the station.'

'Oh, yes . . . stacks. I say, Peggy, you know I've got a birthday sort of coming up.'

'I hadn't forgotten. November the fourteenth, I seem to recall. Do you have anything in mind?'

Of course he had, and it must be rather magnificent if he was going to ask her straight instead of dropping heavy hints as he normally did.

He looked her in the eye. 'Would you mind awfully giving me money this year?'

'No, I don't mind.' But she was surprised. 'You know, I haven't got terribly much but – are you planning to ask everyone for money? Are you going to put it towards something?'

'Yes. I haven't said anything to Mum or Hilda, and the grannies usually send postal orders anyway. I thought I'd try you first.'

'To see how I took it?'

'That's right,' he said, with artless candour. 'Because you never go up in the air when I say the wrong thing.'

Ollie was unlucky to have a birthday that fell just when everyone was saving up for Christmas presents.

'I think it's a good idea – so long as it isn't anything that Mother wouldn't like, not white rats, or an air rifle.'

'Oh, I don't think she'd mind, she just wouldn't understand.'

What on earth could he be after? 'Tell a fellow. You can trust me.'

'I don't suppose you'll know what I'm talking about either,' he said resignedly. 'I'm saving up for a crystal set.'

'Oh, Ollie, how – amazing! I didn't know you were interested in wireless.'

'I didn't think *you* were,' Ollie said. 'I know you borrowed my Morse code but you never talk about it. No one does at home, except Mrs Hendry.'

What had she been missing? All this while she might have been tapping Ollie for information. He must have his set as soon as possible, before he lost interest and found another craze.

'How long have you been saving up?'

'We-e-ell, I've been thinking about it for ages, but you remember that Scout rally I went to?'

'Did you? When was that?'

'Years ago – no, beginning of this month, actually. At the Alexandra Palace. There were fifty thousand of us there, but, you know, everyone couldn't go, even if they wanted to. The Prince of Wales was there.'

'Oh, Ollie, you never told us.'

'Nobody asked. And he addressed us through a *microphone* – you know, fifty thousand people and we could all hear him . . . mostly. And then, in the evening, he said it all again *on air* for the people who didn't go, and the ones with receivers could hear him all over the country. If Scout troops got together round sets they could tune in. Some of our chaps did. I'd almost rather have done that than go to the Ally Pally. You couldn't really see him. So then I thought, Next time, *I'll* have a set. They're setting up a wireless club at school. Hendry and I are going to join.'

'It would be marvellous to have a set at home, though, wouldn't it?' Peggy said. 'Then we could listen to the BBC programmes.'

'What do you know about the BBC?' Ollie demanded. 'Is this why you wanted my Morse code? You're not getting a transmitter, are you?' He looked faintly outraged.

'No, but Ollie, really, I do know what you're talking about. Didn't you know, Irene's brother Ted works for Marconi.'

'What! Why didn't you tell me?'

'You didn't ask.'

Ollie gazed owlishly at her. 'Our family doesn't talk to

each other enough, except about hats and the price of fish.'

'You can talk to me about wireless whenever you like,' Peggy said. 'In fact, I won't just give you something for the set, I'll invest in it. We're – you're – going to need earphones. But you must promise to explain it all, so I know how it works. Oh, crikey! Look at the time.'

'Where?'

Peggy held out her wristwatch. 'I'm going to be late, I've got miles further to go than you.'

They set off at a run in different directions, but the church clock was striking the three-quarters as she turned in at the school gate. 'Oh, *don't* let Hilda be on cloakroom duty.'

Duty prefects lurked at strategic points to intercept latecomers, except in the entrance hall, where only seniors were allowed to come in by the front door. If she went round to the side entrance she would be really, noticeably late; if she nipped in at the front door she might just make it to the cloakroom—

'Where do you think you're going?'

Another sub-prefect, Molly Marchant, was pinning a list on the notice board. Peggy assumed what she hoped was a guileless winning smile.

'Oh, turn a blind eye, Molly, please. I'll be late.'

'You are late. And you know perfectly well that only seniors are allowed to use the front door. Go back and walk – *walk*, mind – to the side entrance. And take an order mark.'

'Molly, *please*. I'll be even later.'

'You should have thought of that before you came sneaking in this way.'

Peggy's irruption through the double doors could hardly be described as sneaking. Surely the main thing was to avoid being late – still, if Molly was determined to be illogical . . .

'Look, I'm in, now. Do let me go through.' She could, of course, cut the ridiculous conversation short by barging past Molly, straight down the corridor; one girl coming in through the wrong door was not going to bring about the collapse of the British Empire. It would be interesting to see if Molly pursued her, hollering.

'Go round the proper way.'

'How can I?' Peggy knew she was sticking her neck out but was too annoyed to care. 'I'm not allowed to go *out* of the front door, either.'

'That's enough of your cheek. Go at once – and you can take a conduct mark too, for arguing.'

What pleasure do they get out of it? Peggy wondered furiously, plodding round to the side entrance since running in the grounds was also forbidden. People like Hilda and Molly, what was the point? They say it's for the good of the school but it's not, it just gives them a feeling of power. If I ever get to be a prefect I'll always turn a blind eye – not to real meanness and spite, but footling things like this.

She was so late, by the time she had taken off her outdoor things and changed into her house shoes, that there was no one left on duty to see her creep out of the cloakroom, but when she gained the door of the form room, Lower V Alpha were rising to line up for prayers. Miss Flower looked at her more in sorrow than in anger.

'Where have you been, Peggy?'

'I was late, Miss Flower. So I came in by the front door to save time and I got sent back round the other way.' Dear Miss Flower, you are strict but fair, everyone says so. See sense.

'I'll have to give you an order mark.'

'Molly Marchant already gave me one, Miss Flower.'

'For being late?'

Lie, you idiot. 'No, for coming in at the wrong door.' But she edited out the conduct mark.

'Well, you know the rules, Peggy. There's no excuse for girls who live as close to the school as you do being late. Order mark.'

Chapter 12

Two order marks in the same morning, in practically as many minutes.

It was almost impossible to get through a term without picking up one or two since the system went against the grain of normal human behaviour, in Peggy's opinion. During this coming week the prefects would be making their hideous sums and deductions ready for the first half totals. Into the equation went the conduct marks – awarded for logic, Peggy thought bitterly, remembering her exchange with Molly Marchant – and the complexities of Commendations and Returns. A Return was a returned lesson, so abysmally bad that it was impossible to mark. Commendations were awarded for exemplary work, or for some unspecified reason by mistresses who just liked the cut of your jib. The mistresses, to be fair, were not much given to overt favouritism; the most you could hope for in that line was to be allowed to carry someone's books, but conduct and order marks were mainly doled out by prefects and some of them were as biased as you please.

The staff could pile on Commendations all they liked; that only got you prizes, but a prefect who had it in for you could make life a misery with order marks.

On Thursday morning, the last day of the half, Peggy checked the form list in the hall and discovered that she had accrued five, and the conduct mark from Molly, which meant an automatic visit to the headmistress at lunch time.

And hasn't *she* got anything better to do? Peggy wondered, standing in the doleful queue outside the head's study door. She had only ever been hauled in once before, years ago, in her second term. Miss Williams had peered at her. 'I'm surprised to see someone from the *Upper Third* coming to me with *five* order marks.' Marjorie Shaw reported a similar reception last year. 'I'm surprised to see someone from the *Upper Fourth* coming to me with *five* order marks.'

Most of the miscreants were from the middle school, infamous for unruly behaviour except in school stories, where people lived in a perpetual Lower IVth, but the girl in front of her was a mere child, and weeping.

'Good Lord, there's nothing to cry about,' Peggy said, stooping down. 'Don't go in there like that.'

The little girl turned round, gulping. 'What will she dooooo?'

'Jaw you, that's all. We don't get beaten or hanged, drawn and quartered. This your first term?'

She nodded, speechless, eyes swollen, nose running, one pigtail chewed to a sodden tassel.

'Five order marks in one half? I don't know how anyone gets through their first term without picking up a couple of dozen. You spend half your time discovering that things that seem perfectly sensible turn out to be the unforgiveable sin. What did you do, walk up the wrong side of the stairs, forget to change your house shoes, eat sweets in the street with your school hat on?'

The child looked awestruck. 'How did you know?'

'I'm clairvoyant,' Peggy said. 'Now, mop up – no, go and wash your face, instanter. And rinse out that plait or it'll clot. I'll take your place if you're not back in time. Kaiser Bill likes you to look decently sorrowful but she won't want you dissolving all over the carpet. Go on, scoot.'

Hilda was passing. 'Did you give that girl permission to leave the line?'

Here's another order mark coming up, Peggy thought. 'Yes, I did. She's in an awful state. I don't see why little kids should be scared half to death because they haven't learned the ropes yet.'

'It's none of your business. When you're in the Sixth you can start giving orders. Meanwhile, you might as well learn to obey them. *Five* order marks—'

'One of which you gave me,' Peggy said. 'Are you going to give me another – for being nice to someone?'

There were six people left in the line and they had all turned and were listening avidly. Only the very littlest ones would not know that Peggy and Hilda were sisters. The rest, as Hilda seemed suddenly to infer, were obviously thinking that they wouldn't want a sister like *her*. She turned and walked away as the mopped-up little girl returned from the cloakroom, less miserable and, unwisely, showing it.

'Go to the end of the line,' Hilda said. 'You're lucky I don't give you another mark for leaving it without permission.'

Peggy shook her head at the child before she could protest that that big girl there had given her leave. Hilda was making quite enough of an ass of herself. It was only a kindness to let her get away before people started hissing. If one did they all would, having got it down to a fine art. It was impossible to pinpoint, it could be done with the lips only slightly apart. Peggy had seen people wound up almost to hysteria by that invisible zephyr of contempt.

The study door opened and a girl came out, looking suitably chastened; another one young enough to take the whole business seriously. Etiquette demanded that she close it behind her, then Peggy must wait a decent interval until the head struck her little brass bell as a signal to the next malefactor. Most people affected to believe that Miss Williams was refreshing herself with a nip of gin between victims.

She went in and stood in front of the desk, hands behind back, feet at ten to two, noticing that on the place where she stood, where everyone must stand, the carpet was losing its pattern under the weight of Sin.

Kaiser Bill stared up at her more in sorrow than in anger. Were schoolmistresses trained to look like that?

'I'm surprised to see someone from the *Lower Fifth* coming to see me with *five* order marks,' she said. They maintained a suitably dreary silence. Did the woman really want to spend her lunch hour doing this? 'Well, Margaret, what have you to say for yourself?'

'Nothing, Miss Williams. I'm sorry.'

'Being sorry is not enough.' Right on cue; being sorry was never enough, but no one ever had the nerve to try not being sorry. 'And I see you have a conduct mark. I find it very distressing that someone in the *Lower*

Fifth should be so unmannerly as to merit a conduct mark.'

'I argued with a sub-prefect,' Peggy said, abruptly exasperated. 'I thought she was being petty – and illogical.'

'My dear–' Miss Williams's voice struck a sincere bass note '– you really are not in a position to judge what is petty and what is not. Rules are here to be obeyed.'

'Sensible rules, yes. But we aren't in the army. Thousands won't die because I came in at the wrong door, to avoid being late. I know I shouldn't have been late but it was the first time for years. Yes, years.'

'It would make no difference if it were the first time ever. You are supposed to be in the form room by ten to nine. Please do not argue with *me*, Margaret. I find your insolence reprehensible. It seems to me that you are developing quite the wrong spirit for a girl at this school. I may have to write to your father.'

'To my mother, Miss Williams.'

'Oh yes. She has a job, has she not?'

'Yes, Miss Williams.' Just like you, you horrible woman. Only it's in a *public* library. Conduct mark for you, Mummy. Working for a living. How *low*.

'Now, I am relieved to see you have no Returns . . . seven Commendations . . . Hmmm.'

Seven Commendations were something of an achievement but Miss Williams, in her carping mood, managed to make them sound like some kind of criminal record.

'And I believe you have seriously upset one of the girls in your form.'

Oh! *Now* they were getting to it. Seven Commendations

and no Returns for mere school work were as nothing. What was she supposed to be at school for?

'I didn't mean to upset her, Miss Williams. She decided to be upset. She needn't have been.'

'Are you a psychologist, Margaret?'

Peggy understood psychologists to be educated people. Miss Williams, by her tone, might have said White Slaver.

'I don't quite understand, Miss Williams.' She was rather pleased with the 'quite'.

'What gives you the right to decide what will upset other people? Dorothy is obviously far more sensitive than you are.'

Peggy had a sudden insight into what Vera Openshaw must have gone through. There were still five girls to see and yet Kaiser Bill was determined to drag out this ridiculous interview for as long as possible, even if it meant missing her lunch. Peggy had not had hers yet. She decided to cut things short.

'I told her all about sex,' she said.

Miss Williams turned a gratifying shade of crimson, vainly casting about for a response.

'Where babies come from,' Peggy explained, helpfully. 'Birth control. It's called contraception these days.'

'This is not the kind of thing I expect my girls—'

'It's the kind of thing we have to know,' Peggy said. 'And please do write to my mother. She thinks I did the right thing. May I go now, Miss Williams?'

The headmistress waved her towards the door.

'Thank you, Miss Williams.'

She went out, closing the door behind her. The

remaining five stared at her anxiously and then with wonder and she realized, as she had done in Gamage's hat department, that she was grinning. Poor brats; Kaiser Bill might lay it on extra thick now, unless she was so prostrated with shock that she could only gibber feebly at them.

There was a kind of penitents' table in the dining room for people who had been detained after lessons ended. It was up at the front, on the slightly raised platform where the staff table stood, so that the rest of the school who stayed to lunch could sit in virtuous smugness and watch the late-comers picking at congealed stew and gelid pudding. All the other tables had a prefect and a sub-prefect to maintain discipline among the remaining eight, who might other-wise riot or put their elbows in the custard. Most people were already finishing their pudding.

Peggy walked up the room to join her fellow outcasts on the platform and serve herself from the dank basin of whatever the stew was calling itself today. The pudding squatted on a plate, hacked about and glistening as if snails had passed over it.

Miss Flower, on the staff table, caught her eye. 'Peggy, you have not excused yourself for being late.'

She stood up again. 'Excuse me for being late, please, Miss Flower.' At this rate she would be gaining a *reputation*.

Adversity had made her hungry. She took a healthy bite of the stew and a violent pain shot through her jaw.

'*Christ!*'

There fell a most deadly silence. Unnoticing, her face feeling as if a nail had been driven through it, Peggy dropped her fork onto the plate with a clatter, clutching her cheek. The clatter was followed by a discreet clink as something else fell out of her open mouth. In the brown swill lay a hard white fragment.

'What on earth is the matter?' Miss Flower was at her side.

Peggy, as the stabbing pain abated to a ferocious ache, poked at the thing in the stew.

'I've broken a tooth.'

'That is no excuse for taking the Lord's name in vain.' Miss Kelsey was weighing in with her two-penn'orth.

'It hurts terribly. May I go and get something for it?'

No, it wasn't a nail, it was a rusty screw, forks of jagged lightning, slow poison . . .

Miss Kelsey, surely out of her mind, was drivelling about finishing her meal first. Even Miss Flower looked annoyed.

'Yes, go along at once, Peggy, and do try to control yourself.'

The stunned silence was breaking into undertones all round the room. 'Did you hear? She swore!'

Hanstead High, under the delusion that only an absence of boarders precluded its being a boarding school, referred to its first-aid post as the Sanatorium, the San. It was a walk-in cupboard attached to the secretary's office and Miss Beaufort, the secretary, administered to the walking wounded from it. She took one look into Peggy's mouth, sat her down and produced cotton wool, clove oil and aspirins.

'What a fang! But how did you do that on *stew*?'

You could speak your mind to Miss Beaufort without wondering how she would take it. She was engaged to be married. The fiancé, Major Gardiner, a dashing type, had been seen on the golf course.

'It was school stew. There was a socking great bone in it.'

The clove oil was working its magic. The pain subsided to a dull, persistent throbbing. Now she could bear to touch the tooth with the tip of her tongue. It felt unpleasantly sharp and ragged, a gaping cave with stalactites.

'Amazing. It was supposed to be rabbit. That looks as if you've been gnawing on dinosaurs. The filling's still there but half the tooth has gone – what bad luck. How soon can you get to the dentist? Who do you go to? I'll ring up.'

'MacMorris. In the High Street.'

'I'll say it's an emergency – what lessons do you have this afternoon?'

'English, French and music. I shan't be able to sing.'

'I should think not. Go and sit on one of those visitors' chairs, while I call.'

The visitors' chairs were upholstered in red plush, one each side of the oak table on which stood the gong. It was made from a brass shell case hanging in a wooden frame, and a decorative plate explained that the wood came from a beam of the cathedral at Ypres, which had been destroyed during the war. Peggy had been noticing it on and off since the day she first came to the school and waited here, with Mother, for her first gracious interview with Miss Williams, who had impressed her then as being very grand but rather nice. She often wondered what the gong was for

– no one ever struck it. They used the ordinary lesson bell for the fire alarm. Things like that were usually given in memory of someone, but there was no name on it. Perhaps it was just in memory of the war, as if anyone would ever forget about it.

Miss Beaufort came out of her office and crossed to where she was sitting. 'Here's a note, Peggy. Give it to whoever's teaching you at a quarter to three. The dentist can see you at ten past, so that will give you plenty of time to get down there. Now, do you want to go and lie down or can you face the English lesson?'

'I can face it, thank you, Miss Beaufort. People will think I'm hiding, otherwise. I'm in trouble.'

'Not like you, Peggy.'

No, it wasn't, actually. She must really be going off the rails today. 'When I broke my tooth I swore. Everyone heard me.'

'Whatever did you say?'

'I took the name of the Lord in vain, Miss Kelsey says. I don't remember what I said, it hurt too much.'

'It's been a long half,' Miss Beaufort said. 'We're all a little frayed at the edges.'

It was only on the way back to Lower V Alpha that Peggy realized that Miss Beaufort had been referring to Miss Kelsey. Frayed at the edges? The woman was threadbare, demonstrably unravelling.

Marjorie saw her leaving the San and came to meet her. 'Are you in agony?'

'It's going off. You shouldn't be in the entrance hall without permission. Lightning will strike you.'

'What was Kelsey on about at lunch?'

'Me swearing. Never mind my tooth.'

'Oh, that cheered us all up,' Marjorie said. 'The swearing, I mean. The sound of a hundred sets of teeth being sucked all at once.'

'I've broken one of mine. I've got to go to the dentist.'

'Right away?'

'In French.'

'Not all bad news, then.'

Mlle Chardin frowned a little when Peggy handed her the note at the beginning of the lesson.

'*Quel dommage*, Peggy. I had better give you your prep now instead of at the end of the lesson.' Typical, Peggy thought. Prep's all that matters. Never mind my tooth. 'You are doing so well this term, it would be a pity to fall behind when you might be at the top of the form by Christmas. Here you are – and also this.' She held out a book in a limp purple cover: *Le Grand Meaulnes*.

Peggy was touched by Mlle Chardin's kind words after she had misjudged her, and by the loan of the book, which she had never expected.

'You may find it harder than you anticipated,' Mlle Chardin said, 'but persevere, do not be disappointed and give up. The fact that you *want* to read it will help. It is a wonderful moment when all those strange sounds and symbols that are a foreign language suddenly become as clear as your own – well, of course I understand, Peggy. I had to learn English, just as you learn French. This book is much loved in France. I'm glad you want to read it.'

'Mam'zelle's a good egg, isn't she?' Marjorie whispered as Peggy sat down, and passed her a note.

If you're not doing anything over the half why not come round to my house on Saturday? 17 Lonsdale Road. 2.30?

Peggy turned it over and wrote, *Yes please, if I live*, and slipped it back. Marjorie read it and smiled, a friendly, open smile; pleased and happy to show it.

Saturdays had once been spent with Dorothy, window shopping, at the films, talking . . . what had they talked about? But now Dorothy lived on the other side of the form room with her little clique. Marjorie had been wrong about that. Lower V Alpha had not split down the middle, it was more like a quarter and three-quarters, and Peggy was in the three-quarters. No one was very shocked by her fearful oath at lunch time and, if word had got around about what she had said to Dorothy, nobody seemed particularly outraged about that, either. Most of them gave her encouraging little waves with their fingers as she left quietly at a signal from Mlle Chardin.

This must be the only way forward, for them all to reject the culture of shock, outrage and affront in the face of things that were not shocking or outrageous, that the school taught alongside French and scripture and algebra. They would have to trust in their own sense of what was right and good.

The corridors and halls were eerily quiet. No one ever walked them during lessons unless they had been sent with a message or, like her, were having to leave early; except members of the VIth Form. The evil demon who had been steering her fate all week, except when Mlle Chardin sent him packing, arranged for Hilda and Joan Sykes to be walking up the corridor as she went down it.

'Where do you think you're going?'

'The dentist,' Peggy said. 'I broke that tooth on the stew at lunch. It's an emergency.'

'How feeble,' Hilda said, 'using that as an excuse to get out of school.'

'Yes,' Peggy said, moving swiftly on. 'Actually, I'm going to the Electric Palace.' Conduct mark coming up.

She could sense Hilda working up a head of steam, but Joan, who sounded as if she were laughing, said, 'Oh, let her go,' and moved serenely on. But Hilda could not let anything go, Peggy knew. There was sure to be a fresh outbreak of criticism when she got home; Mother was working late again this week. In a way it must be easier to deal with the kind of bullies that Ollie came up against. You could see them coming. They left marks.

Hilda would be horrified if anyone suggested that she was a bully but she was, and so, in her way, was Kaiser Bill. Their weapons were soft words, like being beaten up with powder puffs; they left no bruises, it was the knowledge of the beating that hurt.

Chapter 13

The MacMorris waiting room had changed – not very much, but the picture on the wall of the stag at bay had gone. There was a pale patch on the wallpaper and in it hung a smaller painting of a vase of flowers. It was not a very good painting but it was more cheerful than the noble beast facing its grisly doom, just like the patients. It looked as if it had been painted because someone had liked the flowers and had wanted a memory of a happy feeling.

The door from the surgery opened and a woman came out looking quite cheerful.

I've been through this once today, Peggy thought, remembering the glum queue outside Miss Williams's office. If I hadn't been there I wouldn't have been late for lunch and I wouldn't have got that particular spoonful of stew with its booby-trap bone. If I hadn't changed places with that wretched infant I wouldn't have got that spoonful, she would have. But I don't suppose she's got a dud tooth.

'Miss Hutton?'

She went in. There was the chair. There were the instruments. There was MacMorris – no. It wasn't MacMorris. No moustache, fair hair, much younger.

'You're the young lady who broke a tooth?'

Not Scotch, either.

'Do take a seat.' He might have been offering her tea.

184

'Let's have a look . . . oh dear.' Unlike MacMorris he did not expect her to answer while he was clambering about inside her mouth. 'Hurting badly?'

'Like billy-oh.'

'I'm afraid I won't be able to save it. It's . . . um . . . it's not been : . . ah, not very well filled.' He looked abashed at having to apologize for his predecessor's work. He'll be doing plenty of that, Peggy thought.

'It'll have to come out?'

'I'm afraid so. And it's one of those beastly big fellows with roots like parsnips, I'll have to use gas. How much dinner did you get down you before the incident?'

'None, but I had breakfast.'

'Not worth the risk. You mustn't eat before you have a general anaesthetic . . . that means we put you under completely. You've had it before? Can you starve yourself tonight? Have an early tea and come back tomorrow at noon – that'll be a clear twelve hours on an empty stomach. Can you face it?'

He smiled. He was nice. He was not MacMorris.

Peggy smiled back.

'Twelve o'clock, then. There's someone who can come with you?'

That would have to be Hilda again. She would hate to do it but there would be no way of getting out of it without refusing point blank and forcing Mother to take time off from work.

No doubt Hilda would make her pay for it but she was past caring. In less than a day she would be rid of the pain, and the tooth.

* * *

'Of course I can't come with you,' Hilda said. 'I'm spending the half with Phyllis. Her people are taking us to Stratford, we're leaving first thing.'

'I don't want Mother to have to take time off.'

'I don't see why you can't manage on your own. You don't have to have gas, do you?'

'The dentist says I do. He ought to know. And it's not MacMorris any more, there's a new man, Mr Gudgeon. He's nice. I should think he knows what he's talking about.'

'Well, ask one of your friends, if you still have any.' Hilda left the table and gathered up her school bag. 'I'm going to do my prep. Didn't you spin Mother some yarn about doing yours before tea in future? I suppose that was only while you were trying to get round her to let you go to London.'

'I say, she's in a bate, isn't she?' Ollie observed, as the door closed behind her. 'Have you been ragging her at school?'

The atmosphere must be truly poisonous for Ollie to have noticed anything.

'Other way round, Ollie.' She did not want to discuss Hilda's unfathomable hostility with anyone, but Ollie's misdirected sympathy could not pass uncorrected. 'Do you think I'd try and make trouble for her? I can't do anything right. The way she goes on you'd think I'd broken my tooth on purpose, just to cause a fuss. It's so unkind.'

Ollie's owl look was back. 'Jealous,' he said, sagely.

'What of?'

'You're catching up.'

'What with?'

186

'With her. I used to think *I'd* catch up one day, when I was little. I didn't realize you and Hilda were getting bigger too. I thought you were always going to be the same – I mean, when you're a kid, *everybody* looks grown-up – and I'd keep growing until I was as big as you and we'd all be friends. You know when Mum measured us against the door with a knife, when we lived in Bedford Avenue, I saw my marks getting higher each time. I never realized that yours were too.'

'That's right, I'd forgotten. I suppose she forgot as well when we moved. It was the nursery door, wasn't it?'

'Well, I expect she didn't know which door to use when we left off having a nursery. But it would be all of a muddle now, wouldn't it? I'm nearly as tall as you and you're as tall as Hilda. The marks would all run into each other. I dare say I'll be the tallest in the end,' he remarked, with a fatalistic sigh. 'Men are.'

'Sure to be. Daddy was tall. Do you remember him much, Ollie?'

'Not really. He was here, then he wasn't. There, I mean. Bedford Avenue. I go to the war memorial and look at the names and think, That is my father, and I feel sad. I do feel sad because he's dead and he hasn't even got a grave, we don't know where he is. It would be nice to have a dad . . . but it was all so long ago. It was nice having Nana, but it's the same, really. They were people I had when I was little and I don't have them now.' How matter-of-fact he sounded. But it was five years since Passchendaele, almost half his lifetime. 'Look – I borrowed this mag from a boy at school. That's the crystal set.'

187

Peggy examined the picture gravely. It could have been a small sewing machine.

'I'll show you how it works,' Ollie said.

'Do you mind awfully leaving it till tomorrow?' Peggy said. 'I've got this thumping toothache and I haven't washed up yet.'

'It wouldn't have killed Hilda to do that,' Ollie said. 'I'll see to it when I've finished this article.'

'You're an angel, Ollie.'

'Naaah . . . well, just a bit. I've nearly done.'

'You weren't reading it under the table during tea?'

'Yes, and Hilda knew. She didn't say anything, she was too busy jawing you about teeth and things. I wouldn't take it.'

'I have to. Can't you imagine what it would be like if we were quarrelling *all* the time?'

'You are, pretty near. It would clear the air if you had a real set-to. I read this book about a school where if the boys were caught fighting they had to put on gloves and go to the gym and *box*, Queensberry Rules, with a master for referee.'

'I can't see Hilda boxing,' Peggy said. 'But thanks for the washing-up offer – I'll square it with you when I'm quit of this tooth.'

Beyond the window the fog was closing in. It was almost November, the month of chilblains and fireworks. She had already seen Guys on the street and parted with a penny or two.

The last time she had gone to bed early with toothache

it had been summer, she had had to draw the curtains. That had been the first night she had heard the Morse code. It was back now with a vengeance, the tooth stabbing, the signals needling, in and out, in and out, just like a sewing machine.

She could not sleep. Ollie's unexpectedly penetrating words about Hilda came back to her. If Ollie were right she could see things in a different light. She *was* catching up with her sister, not just in height. The two years between them had been a huge gap once and it had always been closing. Irene was two years older than Stella and it made no difference at all. It ought to make no difference to her and Hilda, but Hilda could not see it that way, which was why she clung so fiercely, so desperately, to the trivial differences that the school insisted upon and gave her the right to enforce, where even friendships between girls from different years were frowned upon, as if it were anyone's business but their own. What were people afraid of, Bolshevism? Everyone being equal? Hilda disapproved of Irene and Stella living together instead of going out and finding husbands as if that was their duty. Why? Why shouldn't nice people be nice in their own way? There had been that sly question about the beds in the flat which Hilda had turned into something more than curiosity about furniture.

There was a quiet tap on the door.

'Mummy?'

'Poor love, are you having a bad time? Can I get you anything?'

'No, it's all right. I keep telling myself, this time

189

tomorrow it will be all over. Only another fifteen hours –
then fourteen—'

'I'll meet you there at a quarter to twelve.'

'No, I've been thinking, can't Mrs Hendry come with
me? She wouldn't mind. And when I get home I don't
suppose I'll want to do anything except sleep.'

'Are you sure?'

'Yes. There's no need to come away from work.'

'I wish I had your nerve. I'm a perfect coward about
teeth.'

'No you're not, you're valiant. Can you be valiant about
something else? I'm in trouble at school. Didn't Hilda say
anything?'

Mother sat down on the bed. 'That's why I came up. I'd
have left you to sleep otherwise. She said you'd have something to tell me and were probably lying here worrying
about it.'

Oh, subtle, sneaky Hilda. Peggy sat up. 'I wasn't worrying, Mums, because I don't think it's anything to worry
about. *You* don't think I'm wild and unruly and heading for
the gallows, do you?'

'Of course I do. I lie awake every night praying that
you'll see the path to repentance before it's too late.'

'That's what I thought. I say, Mummy, do we have to go
to church? It's the most awful rot.'

'Peggy!'

'Oh, it *is*. It doesn't make anyone nicer or kinder and we
get enough preaching at school. They really do believe in
the path of repentance there. I've picked up five order
marks this term for things like coming in at the wrong

door. Hilda gave me one herself for laughing in the library – all right, I know we shouldn't, but she only had to tell me to shut up. So, anyway, I had to go and grovel to Miss Williams and it was the usual jaw, "I'm surprised to see someone in the Lower Fifth etcetereteretera . . ." It doesn't matter which year you're in, she's always surprised. You'd think she'd have learned to expect it by now. And then she let on she thinks I'm an evil influence.'

'I hope she didn't use the word evil – about you.'

'No, reprehensible, actually. And do you know what it was all about?'

'I can guess. Dorothy.'

'Got it in one. She said she might have to write to you – that's meant to reduce us to quivering heaps of jelly – and I said that I thought she ought. Write to you, I mean. Do you mind?'

'About you coming in at the wrong door?'

'No, about what I said to Dorothy. I told her. She didn't seem to want to discuss it.'

'So I've to look out for a sulphurous letter that has to be handled with tongs? What about your schoolwork, was she pleased with that?'

'She may have been so overcome with admiration that she was lost for words. I've had seven Commendations so far this term and she never said a thing. You wouldn't think we went to school to *learn*.'

'Things that matter,' Mother sighed. 'Look, I never lose a minute's sleep over you, Peggy, unless you're ill or unhappy.'

'So you'll toss and turn tonight?'

'Are you unhappy? I don't mean fed-up – really unhappy?'

'Not any more. Just toss and turn about the tooth. Tomorrow we can both get a good night's sleep.'

She lay down again. Mother kissed her and went out, closing the door softly. Peggy heard her on the landing telling Ollie to keep the noise down in the attic, although since Ollie had discovered the wonders of electromagnetic waves he had gone very quiet . . . then *dit-ditditditdit-dit-dit*. Her own private radio receiver.

There was the mask, with its own stifling rubbery smell, and then another smell . . . she was lost in Gamage's, where they were having a bargain sale of guinea pigs, thousands of guinea pigs, and a voice said, 'I'm Tom, I've got a message for you.' Then fresh air and another horrible taste in her mouth, blood. A beaker at her lips.

'Rinse. Good rinse. Spit. All over.' Familiar words, but not MacMorris; the new dentist, Mr Gudgeon, and someone else, somewhere in the room. She rinsed and spat a bloody mouthful into the basin. Her tongue went to the tooth, to the absence of tooth, a hole-shaped bruise.

'Well done,' Mr Gudgeon said, bracingly, as if she had taken out the tooth herself. 'Now, have a nice cup of tea and a couple of aspirin when you get home, and only slops today. Tomorrow you'll be as right as rain.'

'Thank you.' She was crying. Why?

'Don't worry, anaesthetic often affects people that way. Nothing to be ashamed of. Now, just sit in the waiting room till you're ready to go. You may feel a bit sick.'

She was looking at the flower painting and Mrs Hendry had an arm around her shoulders.

'There, dear, put your head between your knees. Feeling faint? I'm not surprised.'

Much more comforting than Hilda telling her not to be feeble.

'How does it feel?'

'As if I've been socked in the jaw with a boxing glove with a brick in it.'

'I had all mine out when the kiddies started coming. Saves time and money later on. Those big teeth go down a long way,' Mrs Hendry said. 'Never mind, mouths heal ever so quickly if they're clean. Spit's the best medicine. Jesus used it in the Bible.'

'Did he? I don't remember.'

'Healing somebody, a blind man, wasn't it? Spat in the dust and put the mud on his eyelids. It always sounded very mucky to me but I suppose it was Holy Spit.'

Miss Kelsey had always skimmed over that bit, as with other pathological parts of the New Testament, like the woman with an issue of blood, twelve years. Now Peggy knew why.

'Better? Let's get you home then.'

They walked back slowly through the foggy streets, across the park, past the war memorial. No one was playing there today.

'Now for that cup of tea,' Mrs Hendry said, when they got in. 'Do you want to go to bed and I'll bring it up?'

'No thanks, I'll just sit in the parlour,' Peggy said. 'I can always lie down if I feel swimmy.'

The parlour was warm and quiet. Mrs Hendry had lit the fire as soon as they came in. Peggy drank her tea cautiously and lay back on the couch. She heard Mrs Hendry leave. A motor van went by, then a delivery dray, but it was very quiet apart from the fire, ticking and sighing as it settled down to a red glow.

She closed her eyes. It was not just quiet but silent; silent outside her head and in it. Where was the *dit–dit–dit* of the Morse code, the tinny voice?

She could hear music, the Schubert rondo. At any moment now the signals would begin, *dit-dit-ditdit-dit*. She was almost at the point where she could decode what they were telling her, especially now that she knew where they were coming from. She might even pick up distress signals, from ships at sea, like the *Volturno* ablaze in the Atlantic.

But the Schubert went on, uninterrupted, there were no signals, no messages from beyond, or even from some amateur in the next street perhaps; no broadcast from Chelmsford or Writtle. What had happened, what had become of her private radio receiver? And then, in a flash of relief mixed with disappointment, she knew what had become of it. It was not only her tooth that Mr Gudgeon had removed at twelve o'clock.

Before he went out in the morning Ollie slipped his wireless magazine under her door.

Peggy, left to sleep late in deference to her tooth, or the lack of it, and the fact that there was no school, took it down to read over breakfast. It was packed with small print, diagrams and advertisements. Called *Amateur Wireless* it was evidently intended for people like Ollie and the Hendry brothers and Brian Summersby, although not for Ted, the professional.

And not for her. She did not understand any of it. This was the future and she was going to be left behind. All very well; she and Ollie would buy the kit and Ollie would build the crystal set and she would listen in, but it wasn't enough. She had to know how it worked – everyone would have receiving sets soon, the kind with valves, Ted had told her, and *Amateur Wireless* was showing her what they would look like. If the Huttons ever had one of these magic boxes in the house she wanted to know what would be going on inside it. Valves, capacitors, induction, oscillation, frequencies, anodes, cathodes . . . She flipped through the pages . . . sinusoids . . . Why weren't they learning about this at school?

But soon, who could need school? If all these wonders came to pass, anyone could learn anything, they would not need money or scholarships, schools, universities. No one could stop them learning because they were poor or because they were girls. There need be no more Dorothys, frightened and ignorant. It would be the end of ignorance.

She could hear Mrs Hendry in the sitting room, cleaning round the fireplace. An idea began to sprout, almost unnoticed, and then take root. She went next door.

'Mrs Hendry?'

'I didn't hear you come down. How's the tooth?'

'Bliss. Just a bit of a bruise. Do you remember, ages ago, we were talking about crystal sets?'

Jan Mark

'David's got on to that now,' Mrs Hendry said.

'So Ollie was saying. The two of them have got quite pally this term. Well, I've got a friend, and his brother works for Marconi. You know, I think we could start our own wireless club, don't you? I know you haven't got electricity but we have. We could share.'

'What, you mean the boys bring their doodahs round here? What'll your mum say to that?'

'Shouldn't think she'd mind a bit,' Peggy said, 'and Hilda can just stew. Anyway, we're sort of in Maurice's debt. Ollie was getting knocked about at school and he put a stop to it. Don't say anything yet, I have to plan this.'

'So you do think she'll mind. Watch your feet with that black-lead.'

'Oh, it's not that, but I can see what might happen. I'll have the idea and set it all up and then get left out.'

'I know; they'll expect you to make the tea.'

'Not this child. They can make their own tea. I'm going up to the library now. Do we need anything from the shops?'

'We could do with some more Bluebell polish if you're passing the ironmonger's, and we're running a bit low on candles. Best to get a stock in now with it getting dark so early. You never know when there'll be a power cut. And matches, while you're about it.'

When she went out it was raining, the dank, persistent drizzle that always seemed to set in at the end of the month, ready to douse bonfires and spoil fireworks. Peggy called in at the bakery and at the ironmonger's for the candles and polish.

'Anything else, miss?'

Mrs Hendry had asked for matches.

'No thank you,' Peggy said. She went out and walked back towards the post office, where the ex-serviceman was standing against the wall for shelter. He had a square of oilskin over his tray.

'Six boxes of safety matches, please.'

While he dug them out she stood back and deliberately read the placard, the short story of his loss.

MY BROTHER JOHN FELL AT MONS
MY BROTHER GEORGE WAS GASSED AT CAMBRAI
MY BROTHER JAMES WAS LOST AT PASSCHENDAELE
'AND I ONLY AM ESCAPED ALONE TO TELL THEE.'
1 JOB 15

'My father died at Passchendaele too,' she said. She saw his surprise that she had spoken. He was no more surprised than she was. 'How did you escape – to tell?'

'I should have been there myself, but I'd already lost this.' He touched his empty sleeve. 'The whole company was wiped out.'

'I'm sorry.' What a meagre thing to say, but how could she not say it?

'Me too, miss. About your dad. Officer, was he?'

'No, a rifleman. He joined up as a private but they'd just made him a corporal. Alan Hutton, Twelfth Battalion. What's your name – I mean, I know your brothers'.'

'Joseph. Joe Castle.'

'Thank you, Mr Castle.' They smiled at each other. 'I

expect I'll see you again soon. We always need matches.'

I could have done that ages ago, she thought, moving on. What was I afraid of, that he'd think I was talking down to him? That was just what she had been afraid of, she had seen too much of the Ladies' Benevolent being fearfully *nice* to people. As soon as she opened her mouth he had known she was officer class – only she wasn't. She was a rifleman's daughter. She was so proud of having been able to say that.

The rain came down harder as she headed uphill towards the library, where the lights were on and the stoves were lit. Mother said the place always filled up on wet days.

She looked surprised when Peggy walked in and they had to converse in whispers across the desk under the enormous SILENCE sign.

'I didn't expect to see you.'

'I'm feeling top-hole now. You'd never know there'd been anything wrong. I'm going to advertise Mr Gudgeon.'

'Have you come in just to get dry?'

'No, I want books. Have you got anything on wireless?'

'We should have, why? Did Ollie get you to come in? He could have asked me.'

'He's told you about it, then. No, I want to read up on it myself.'

A crabby-looking woman at one of the tables glared at them accusingly.

'She's going to give us an order mark. Where are they?'

'In the science section – the three hundreds.'

'Thanks – oh, I bought you a sticky bun for elevenses. Be careful, the sticky's coming through the bag.'

The crabby woman coughed meaningly. Peggy smiled sweetly as she passed on her way to the science shelves. Science. The nearest they got to science at school was botany, since plants could be trusted to do nothing that would bring a blush even to Miss Kelsey's maidenly cheek.

There were no books on wireless but she could see that there ought to be. Almost a whole shelf was empty. Everyone in town was getting wired-in to wireless. She would have to put in a reservation and meanwhile pin down Ollie with his magazines and make him explain; or contrive another meeting with the Summersbys.

This reminded her of something that had to be done. She went back to the desk.

'Nothing there?'

'They've all been borrowed.' A threatening cough came from behind her. 'Look, I've just remembered, I have to write a letter. Could you thieve me a sheet of library paper and an envelope?'

She sat at a table in the reference room, where the rule of silence was observed like Holy Writ. The sheet Mother had given her was twice the size of ordinary paper, with HANSTEAD URBAN DISTRICT COUNCIL PUBLIC LIBRARY printed across the top. Stella would think it was official, until she started reading. Peggy started writing.

October 28th 1922

Dear Stella,

I have to tell you this immediately. I had my tooth out yesterday, the one that was aching. We have a lovely new dentist who has put a decent picture on the wall in the waiting room. You must tell all your Hanstead friends to go to him. Anyway, for the first time since I had the beastly thing filled, I didn't hear any Morse last night, or this morning, so I've realized now where it was coming from. You'll never believe this, but I must have been picking up radio waves in my filling. It only started after I had it done, and now it's gone the Morse has gone too. I'm pretty sick in a way because I was almost about to be able to decode it, but it is a relief to know what was happening.

I'm going shares with Ollie in a crystal set instead, so we can listen to real broadcasting, but that's only a beginning. Brian says that before long we shan't be sending just sounds through the air but pictures as well, television. I mean to get into radio somehow. School's useless. Any suggestions? You couldn't work on Granny Holt, could you, to let me go to the girls' grammar in Croydon? If I could get a scholarship, and I think I could, she wouldn't have to pay fees any more, just the train fares. I'll have to act soon because if I stay at Hanstead High all the brains I have will turn to mush and trickle out of my ears. I think they would like to throw me out anyway.

I'm sorry about the Morse, that it wasn't messages from the other side, though in a way it was, only not from the past but from the future. Brian told me radio waves are electromagnetic like light. Light goes on for ever. Just think, we could send messages out into space, on carrier waves, and perhaps one day they'd be heard on the other side of the universe . . .

Afterword

Peggy's private radio receiver is not as unlikely as it may seem. As a teenager, in the 1950s, I was plagued at night by the sound of high-speed Morse transmissions. I had no idea where they were coming from, or why I could hear them, and it was only many years later that I read a letter in a electronics magazine, describing the same sensation and suggesting that filled teeth might pick up radio waves. That was the basis for this book. By coincidence, just as I was finishing it I read an article on the subject in *Fortean Times*, the journal of unexplained phenomena. What Peggy and I were experiencing is called electrophonics, the conversion of electromagnetic energy into sound. Obviously, this is what a real radio receiver is doing, but there is evidence that people can pick up radio or microwaves through shrapnel fragments, hair, wire-framed glasses and . . . dental fillings.